IZ~ THE IZZY STORY

Book 1 Encounters

By

Ddwlem

TELEMACHUS PRESS

This is a work of fiction. Any reference to characters, names, incidents, organizations, and dialogue in this novel are either the products of the author's imagination or are used fictitiously.

IZ~ THE IZZY STORY: BOOK 1, ENCOUNTERS

Copyright © 2015 DDWLEM, LLC. All rights reserved. No part of this book may be used or reproduced by any means, graphic, electronic, or mechanical, including photo copying, recording, taping or by any information storage retrieval system either in existence or yet to be created without the prior written permission of the author except in the case of brief quotations embodied in critical articles and reviews.

The publisher does not have any control over and does not assume any responsibility for author or third-party websites or their content.

Cover and illustrations designed by Chalice Mitchell

Published by Telemachus Press, LLC
7652 Sawmill Road, Suite 304
Dublin, Ohio 43016
941-504-5496
www.TelemachusPress.com

Contact DDWLEM, LLC:
Business email: theizzystory@gmail.com
Twitter: @IZTheizzystory
Facebook: www.facebook.com/IZTheIzzyStory
Website: http://www.theizzystory.com
YouTube: https://www.youtube.com/user/theizzystory

ISBN 978-1-941536-41-4 (eBook)
ISBN 978-1-941536-42-1 (paperback)
ISBN 978-1-941536-76-6 (hardback)

Version 2015.04.07

Printed in the United States of America
10 9 8 7 6 5 4 3 2 1

Table of Contents

Dedication

To researchers around the world who uncompromisingly dedicate their lives to developing vaccines that prevent infectious disease.

Credits

A team of young, talented creators have added vision, voice, and sound to Iz~. Their artistry has inspired us to not only produce an eBook, and paper editions of our story but also to simultaneously provide the audio version. They have devoted countless hours to helping us make Book 1 of IZ~ a unique and entertaining reality. Please feel free to enjoy the latest of their talent on our website at: http://www.theizzystory.com, our YouTube channel at www.youtube.com/theizzystory/videos; and if you too enjoy the story please like us on our Facebook page at: https://www.facebook.com/IZTheIzzyStory.

Artist: Chalice Mitchell

Composer: Steven A. Gearhart

Video Production: Pixel After Pixel

3D Artist: Denisa Kuldová

Voice Actor for Multiple Male Voices and Audio Engineer: Roy Kelly

Voice Actor for Multiple Female Voices: Patricia True

Voice Actor for Carys: Morgan Fraser

Social Media Manager: Morgan Trousdale

A special note of thanks to Jonathan Brazee, content editor, who gave us the cutlass to slash out the dead wood and the battle cry for action.

We are eternally grateful to Louise M. Reiter, research and copy editor, for her expertise in literary style, her sharp eye for detail, and her helpful suggestions that enhanced our story's readability.

Acknowledgments

Our heartfelt gratitude goes to the following people, institutions, and organizations for volunteering their time and expertise. Their contributions have wowed us, humbled us, and brought us many times back to the drawing board.

John Alastick, Jesper Bartholdy, Bournemouth University, Cheetah, Alain Chenciner, Barry Cooper, Sheila Dennehy, James Donald, Veljko Dmitrašinović, Damian Evans, Fiction Writers Workshop of Mercer County Library Lawrenceville, New Jersey, Alex Filippenko, Anna Fraser, Andrew Fraser, Dawn Fraser, John Fraser, Tobias Grace, Chris Greenstock, Adam Gwilt, Judy Hoffman, Rich Hoffman, Jeanette Horner, Rodney Horner, Jacaranda Writer's Group of Venice Florida, Tina Bartley Martin, Esther Michaels, Judy McCann, Robin Michaels, Borge Nielsen, Jonna Nielsen, Bonnie North, Hanson North, Hugh O'Byrne, Sydney Olander, Rona Parry, Peter Vang Petersen, George Repella, Joan Repella, Princeton University, Milovan Šuvakov, Howell Sweat, Dimitri Tsatsaris, Robert Vanderbei, Sylvain Verdier, Peter Walker, Claudia Whitehurst, John J. Whitehurst, Tim Whitehurst, Hal Wittlinger, Marilyn Wittlinger, Donna Wolfe, and Sarah Wright.

For a detailed and updated description of each person's contributions please see our Acknowledgments page on our website:

http://www.theizzystory.com/acknowledgments/

Prologue

Our past holds many secrets clouded in myth. Consider this possibility: suppose an advanced civilization was burdened with a pandemic plague created by genetic research. Further complicating the issue, the citizens of that civilization banned all geneticists from pursuing research that would lead to a cure for the disease!

What if the remaining option of the well-intended geneticists was to take their research to a distant world, only to discover the civilization of that world was less advanced then they in technology and communication? Would the appearance of these alien visitors become the subject of an oral tradition in that distant world? Do such legends exist in our world today?

What if those geneticists had left behind a valuable object? Would the inhabitants of that less-sophisticated society recognize its value and treasure it? Is it possible that such an object may be found today, not only among the pages of this story, but in an unexplored part of our Earth?

IZ~ THE IZZY STORY

Book 1 Encounters

Chalice

Chapter 1
ATTACK

E Two Two! E Two Two! E Two Two!

Chico Quwattle dashed out of the conference room, leaving Izzy to scramble onto Dorf 's back while trailing crumbs from his quickly abandoned congratulatory treat.

The emergency code created another path of glial cells around newly forming neurons in Izzy's brain. He climbed onto Dorf 's shoulder, twisted his neck to make eye-to-eye contact, and glialpathed, *Izzy can help. What can he do? What can Izzy do?*

Dorf Tzeus jerked his head around and saw Izzy's pleading gaze. The geneticist had been sending lock-down signals to his files through his organic wrist Dyzzleberry Communicator, commonly referred to as a DB.

"Extreme urgency, Iz." Dorf lowered his voice. "They're breaking in. Here, get inside my shirt." Dr. Tzeus pulled back the neck of his shirt. "Flatten out against my back and keep that tail of yours hidden. We've got trouble. Don't let them see your face."

Izzy was happy to hide, or make an attempt at it. The banana-sized feline/iguana scuttled backward inside the shirt's stretchy fabric, his long fur-ridged-tail nesting at Dorf 's waist.

The tall, soft-spoken geneticist ignored Izzy's little padded feet as the creature repositioned himself. Dorf tightened his shoulder muscles in an effort to disregard the tickle of whiskers on his back as he reported to his boss. "I've secured the records for ABMR-Virus Cure and deleted them from all work centers."

Ponce Heidon, who'd been tracking the invaders' movements from the security wall monitors, turned and nodded his approval. Beads of perspiration ringed his smooth, hairless head. "They've destroyed the labs in Building 2 and are headed this way," he told the others in the room. "Robar and Phed, block the entrance. Cimi, make …"

Pop!

Cimi Nuja had anticipated Dr. Heidon's request and prefaced her response by cracking a bubble with the wad of gum in her mouth. "All technology locked, Director." Ponce Heidon knew Cimi was on top of things when he saw that the tuft of hair at the top of her otherwise bald head had remained blue as she continued concentrating on her security-breach problem.

Cimi tapped out PHI104 on her DB. No response. She pressed it again. "Where's Chico? Did anyone see where she went? She's not responding to my path!" Her tuft of hair faded to pale yellow.

No one answered Cimi's emotional appeal.

An explosion blasted the vaulted entrance that separated the conference center from the laboratory. Robar and Phed were thrown across the room. Phed's light body slid down the silicon-surfaced table, and Robar landed with a thud on the marble floor at Ponce's feet.

Cimi dashed under the table. Sensitive to loud noises, she instinctively tore off two hunks of gum and plugged her ears. She saw Phed's foot hanging over the table's edge and pulled it so hard that the bewildered PhD candidate had no choice but to join her.

Ponce and Dorf, engulfed in a piercing hail of shards, didn't see the intruders enter. Five uniformed shapes appeared before the stunned scientists. Behind them, a throng of ordinary-looking protesters barricaded the cavernous entrance. They pointed small weapons at Ponce, Dorf, and Robar—that appeared to be light-emission guns, weapons designed to vaporize organic material with one well-placed shot. Robar quickly righted himself.

A broad-shouldered female addressed the PHI director, "Ponce Heidon, that is 'The Great Dr. Ponce Heidon.'" Her military jacket sparkled with medals and announced her undisputed superiority over the others flanking her.

She singled out Ponce. Two soldiers yanked his arms behind him then forced him to the floor. As they dragged Ponce across the rubble, he screamed in pain.

Dorf rushed to Ponce's aid and flashed one riveting burst of his Stunfire before a blow to his head sent him toppling to the floor.

Izzy streaked out from under Dorf 's shirt onto his master's fallen body. Displaying a fearsome posture, he felt a primordial tingle envelope his body. His leathery skin puffed up and unfolded a newly found dewlap. Power pumped through every cell. He humped his back and raised the ridge of black shiny fur so that it stood erect from his head to the tip of his tail. No longer soft and silky, each strand of fur had become as rigid as steel, the tips needle-sharp points. Izzy's fur was peppered with brilliant green spear-shaped filaments that stood straight among the stiff black hairs like iridescent emerald daggers, his dewlap a fiery flashing sail.

He tilted his head up, opened his jaws, and bared his teeth. A web of scaly skin fanned out on both sides of his mouth creating a chasm that intensified a sound from deep within. It began as a low gurgle, then raced to a hissing roar, finally elevating to a siren of torturous pain. The sound shocked every nerve fiber and every muscle of both the good and the bad. Those who were standing fell to the ground.

There was no crying out as icy shards of life seeped through the ravaged victims' veins. They lay frozen struggling to breathe. Their bodies shivered uncontrollably while their minds conjured up visions of their own violent deaths; each death was more horrifying than the next, cycling without end.

Throat muscles paralyzed. No terror could be manifest in screams of agony, only that of agonizing silence.

Izzy closed his mouth. Then he shut his eyes and collapsed.

For the longest of moments, not a sound could be heard in the ruins of the hallowed scholarly space. Then slowly, the ridged forms of the once-angry protesters began to relax.

Blood sluggishly pumped back into withered veins and throat muscles began to flex. Nerve fibers calmed.

"It's a monster!" the once emboldened attackers screamed in fear. "They've created a monster!"

They stumbled and fell, crunching through the broken plexi, rock, and metal. Some were still blinded, and they desperately clawed over each other to escape.

Cimi eased herself out from under the table and unplugged her ears. Pulling out the sticky mass, she had to be careful not to entangle the gum in her huge hoop earrings. She felt fine, totally unaffected by the horrendous noise. Glancing around, she noticed her friends were still unconscious. They were the closest to Izzy, especially Dorf.

Looking down at the wads of moist blackness in her hand, Cimi murmured, "It must be the gum." *Maybe my saliva chemically altered the effect of Izzy's attack,* she thought. *I'll have to test this later.* She pocketed it for safekeeping, then popped a fresh cube into her mouth.

Kneeling by Dorf, Cimi was relieved to find he was still breathing, but there was a nasty lump on the back of his head. She pathed for help. *CRTA1-15 Triage,* repeatedly tapping the emergency icon on her DB. Frustrated, she yelled, "Don't tell me they've killed the signal!" Cimi looked over and saw Phed stirring. "Phed, you OK?" *What a stupid question,* she thought, *of course he isn't OK. No one's OK, Not even Izzy who saved us is OK …*

Placing her hand on Izzy's back, she began to stroke the little creature's furry ridge. His fur was soft but moist, unlike its normal fluffy dryness. Cimi picked him up and murmured, "Oh, you poor sweet thing." She cradled him with both arms and gave him a squeezy hug.

His fur fluffed up and his big blue eyes opened to stare at Cimi's widest-ever smile. He noticed that a strand of hair had fallen over her eye. It was not its normal Olym yellow.

"How'd you do that, Iz? You saved our lives!"

Izzy squeezed away enough to push his face close to hers.

Daddy Tzeus, he pathed, *Daddy Tzeus, what's wrong with Daddy Tzeus?*

"He's going to be OK, Iz. He had a shock and you saved his life. I'm going for help."

She carried Izzy over to Phed, who struggled to sit up.

"Izzy, where'd you get that sound? Wicked! It's wickedly wonderful!" He thrust out both hands. "I'll take him, Cim. You go for help, I'm still woozy! Come on, Iz, you and I will stay right here."

He crossed his legs and held Izzy close.

Cimi reprogrammed the communication module on her DB and sent a message to Phed.

"Got it, Cim," he said, confirming the connection.

"Good, we're back in contact. The system's down but at least we can path each other."

You forgot about Izzy!

Cimi, surprised by Izzy's glialpath, looked down and saw him stretched out on Phed's shoulder, straining his body to catch her attention.

Izzy's signal's strong. It's not down. He wants to help. What can Izzy do?

Chapter 2
SKEPTICAL

You're probably skeptical that a combination of cat, iguana, and Authairian DNA could develop into a banana-sized creature with a powerful acoustic weapon … a weapon that is capable of preventing a massacre.

I was skeptical too, and I'm not an Earthling like you. I'm that feline/iguana from Planet Authair. That's why I'd like you to take a moment and hear my story.

The invasion at the genetics laboratory on Planet Authair happened a long time ago. I'm much older now. Let's see, I'm 130 years old by your standards, and my mind's still sharp. Nobody really knows how long Authairian feline/iguanas live, and I want you to know my personal remarks before I start forgetting them.

My first attack was spontaneous. I didn't understand what was happening to me. All I knew at that moment was my friends' lives were being threatened. I'd been hiding inside Dorf 's shirt when he was knocked unconscious. Suddenly a surge of power deep within my body welled up. I felt an uncontrollable urge to help. Something pulsated through my organs pounding and pounding. My vision blurred, I couldn't hear anything, and I struggled for air. Suddenly, everything went black.

I awoke to a gentle hand on my head. Cimi was standing over me.

"What'd you do, Iz? That was Olymfab! You saved our lives!" Cimi was careful not to let her huge earrings get in the way when she picked me up and gave me a big squeezy hug.

That's when I saw the strand of hair drooping above her eye. Her normally bright yellow tuft of hair had turned white. Something was wrong.

As I clung to her shoulders, I looked down and saw Daddy Tzeus. I call Dorf "Daddy Tzeus" because we share a bloodline. Dorf 's blood had mixed with the chemicals on the lab floor that ended up being me. But, that's another story … You can ask Phed all about that. He'd taken minute by minute records of my development because his job was to take care of me until I died.

They never expected me to live longer than a few hours.

Anyway, I'm wandering. Let's get back to the attack.

When I first gained consciousness, I felt a deep emptiness inside. Dorf was unconscious, Ponce and Robar were not moving, and Phed was moaning. I sensed Cimi was scared, and I never saw her afraid of anything before this. I couldn't understand why all my friends were lying on the floor, except Cimi.

Remember, I was only seven months old then and desperately needed comforting myself.

Later they told me how I'd transformed into a fierce-looking monster during the attack and what a nerve-bursting sound I'd made. I liked it when Phed said, "It was wicked, wonderfully wicked!" His eyes were huge. That's when I knew the wicked I'd done was a good wicked.

If what I've just told you hasn't removed your skepticism about me, there's one more event that may change your mind.

It started with Kurl Tszargon. Kurl's an astrophysicist from Authair. He'd been so successful at searching for life on other worlds that Dr. Ponce Heidon asked him to join the ABMR-Virus team. By the time I was six months old, I'd learned everything about Kurl Tszargon. I wanted to meet him in person.

This was before I knew about my acoustic weapon.

As I rapidly developed, a remarkable communication system evolved in my brain. I had no vocal chords but people could understand me, and I could hear and understand them. Highly developed neurons with specialized glial cells sent my messages to them by tapping into their brains' electro-chemical pulses. Their brains, in return, interpreted that as a spoken message. People understood what I'd "path" or send them. I don't ever remember learning to do this; it came naturally. As you can hear, I still communicate by glialpathing.

I learned that Kurl was a chess master, a Kan-Du master, and a brilliant astrophysicist with a sterling reputation on Authair. I wanted to be his friend and play chess, like I did with Phed. But, Kurl didn't want to be my friend. In fact, he called me a mutant lizard. He wasn't present during the attack, and he didn't believe Ponce's report about my paralyzing powers.

As young as I was then, I had developed an opinion about Kurl: I think it was extremely difficult for him to admit he made a mistake about me. I figured I would need to perform 'to the extreme' for him to respect me as a member of the team.

On our trip to MBG2I, otherwise known as Earth, I did a few things that impressed Kurl. I wasn't trying to impress him, but because it was a matter of life, death, or tuna broccoli treats. I was going for the tuna broccoli and, luckily, we got life, and I got the treats.

As an added bonus, Kurl played chess with me.

Now, Kurl doesn't easily make friends … it's more like non-enemies. After the chess match, I became his non-enemy. I was happy to be a non-enemy. That meant Kurl no longer thought of me as a "mutant lizard" and started calling me "Izzy." Sometimes he'd even shorten it to "Iz." I was allowed to call him "Master Kurl."

We'd been on MBG21 for four-and-a-half years. One day Kurl asked me if I'd like to see his laboratory on the ship *Graviton 1*. I was so excited that I stood up on my hind legs and tried not to jump up and down. I even held my hands behind my back when I glialpathed, *Izzy would consider that an honor, Master Kurl.*

"Meet me at the control central tube tomorrow at full sun," he replied in his matter-of-fact way.

The next day we met at the tube and descended to a lower level inside *Graviton 1*. Kurl led me into a huge triangular space filled with an array of geometrically shaped machines. I was too small to see much of anything from the floor.

"Climb up on the table," he said, tapping it with his hand. "You'll be able to see the operating mechanisms of the machines."

I jumped up. *Wow! This is awesome!* I'll bet my eyes were about the size of my head. I'd even prepared a thank-you speech. Standing tall with my hands clasped in front of me, I looked straight at him and glialpathed, *Master Kurl, this is an honor and a pleasure to be a guest in your laboratory. I would like to thank you for this opportunity*. I don't know if he heard me, since he replied before I had time to take a breath. Clearing his throat, he straightened up his shoulders and said, "Izzy, I made you a gift; I want you to have it as my way of saying 'I'm sorry.' You should know that Ponce, Chico, and Cimi all contributed something to make this gift. I used some of the equipment in this laboratory to create it."

He nodded his head toward what I later learned was the plasma furnace, and with his hands behind his back continued without a pause. "I'm sorry I called you a mutant lizard and refused to play chess with you. Mostly, I'm sorry I hurt your feelings. I hope you'll accept this gift as an expression of my friendship."

Then Master Kurl revealed what he had been hiding behind his back. He handed me a sparkling white object. Its dish-like shape displayed a golden rim and an inner ring of ruby red. In the center were black sparkling letters that spelled my name, I-Z-Z-Y. It was just the right size for one of my tuna broccoli treats.

For Izzy? An apology gift for me?

It was beautiful. I gripped its shiny gold rim with both hands and turned it round and round inspecting the curious design of symbols that decorated the plate's outer lip.

Kurl explained that the symbols were a story about my adventures from the time I'd been discovered on the laboratory floor to the present. My challenge was to decipher the script and follow my story.

My gift's a puzzle? Izzy loves puzzles! I sat down with the plate on Kurl's lab table. *Look! That symbol's Izzy.* I pointed to a squiggly line attached to what looked like the letter M. *That's me!*

Kurl abandoned the lab tour when he realized that all I wanted to do was solve the puzzle and read the story—my story.

***

Daddy Tzeus! Look! It's an apology gift from Master Kurl! I surprised Dorf by jumping onto the console at the command center and holding the plate up to his face for closer inspection.

"Wow, that's really special, Iz! Did you know those symbols were made with Ponce's ancient font?"

Dorf explained the whole story about how Ponce and Kurl had worked together unlocking the meaning of the last two symbols before Kurl stamped the message onto the plate.

Then he told me that Chico was fighting mad when she had to give Kurl her favorite chef s knife because of some secret project he was working on.

I felt bad about that, so I showed Chico the plate.

"That's what he used my ceramic carver for? Kurl didn't tell me he was going to melt it down! That's a work of art, Iz. Look how the ceramic sparkles. He's put a special coating over the surface. Wow! Every symbol's perfectly placed. You must mean a lot to him."

As Chico examined it further, she said she couldn't wait to put a fresh treat into it.

"Izzy, what's that you've got?" Cimi asked. She never wanted to be left out of a good story, so she picked me up and put me in her lap. I handed my gift to her. "That's Olymfab, just Olymfab!" She held the plate up and studied the designs.

"I knew Kurl must've had a good reason to take almost all the gum I had. I even told Ponce about it, and he said to give it to Kurl. Ponce also told me not to worry about having enough gum to protect us from another one of your attacks. Now I get it, Iz. Do you remember when I told you the multiwalled carbon nanotubes make the Double Trouble Bubble Gum black? How clever of him to use the nanotubes in the gum to make the black ink for the lettering. That's some special gift."

She tapped her finger on each symbol around the plate. "Tell me what these mean, Iz. I know you've deciphered them by now. Wait! Let me guess." Cimi pointed to the character that looked like a tail in front of the letter M. "That's you! That means 'Izzy'! Oh, this is fun!"

Even Cimi had been impressed.

You can understand why Kurl's gift became my most cherished possession. I took it everywhere with me. It fit snuggly in a pocket of my vest, and that's how I lost it. I had that precious plate for about a month when Dorf asked me, "Izzy, want to join me? I've got to warn Illiachus about the approaching brown dwarf sun."

I was frightened. We'd all been preparing for an early departure from MBG21 because, according to Kurl, the brown dwarf that previously damaged our ship's computer processing unit was now going to pass dangerously close to Earth. To warn Illiachus in time, we had to travel over a large body of water rather quickly.

I put my plate in its custom-sized pocket and glialpathed. *At your service, Daddy Tzeus! Izzy wants to help.*

***

Dorf and I arrived at the Island of Caves. We had no time to wait for Illiachus' arrival. Dorf found some pliable earth that he worked into a ball, then flattened it out and drew a message in pictures. The pictures showed Illiachus where to go for safety.

Just as we'd placed the message against a rock where Illiachus could easily find it, a sudden volcanic tremor shook the ground. Sulfurous fumes belched out from cracks around our feet burning our eyes and searing our lungs. I remember hanging on Dorf's neck as he ran.

Flying debris hit us from every direction. Bruised and bleeding, we made it to the safety of the terra shuttle. As we lifted off the surface, I was horrified. My vest pocket was torn and empty. Kurl's precious gift was gone!

***

That was a long time ago. Even now, images flash through my mind upon my awakening. I see a small sparkling object held curiously in many hands. Gnarled old hands pass it on to youthful hands that cling to it. Finally it takes a strange and rocky journey to find itself in hands that reverently trace over its design and copy its symbols.

These images feel like an organic presence of energy; energy that's traveled through the vastness of space to convince me that Kurl's gift has been found.

I'm convinced, but I've changed my mind about you. Of course you're still skeptical. Earthlings need facts to believe in visitors like me.

Chapter 3
DISCOVERY

Part 1

South England, 2000 CE

The summer day had been full of rain. Heavy bursts of water pelted the landscape then slowed to a misty shower only to repeat the drenching pattern. It wasn't until seven-ish that a hazy sun appeared through the clouds promising time enough to pop Tasy in the hand-me-down Peugeot and go for a jog. Tasy was her pet terrier and she was Dee, an archaeology student eager to get on with the daily jog around Stonehenge. Maybe it was her intimacy with the site that drew her there, or just the convenience. The house she roomed at was nearby in Laverstock, and this was the longest stretch for jogging in the area. Reason enough.

Dee parked the car on the southwestern end of the earthen road. The usual small family campers were nowhere to be seen. All the tour buses and employees were gone. The visitors' parking gate was locked and it was peaceful. Evening trekkers could still access the walking paths, but today the rain had kept them away. The traffic along the A344 and the 303 was all but nonexistent. She looked forward to the solitude and exercise.

"Just a minute, Tas. Hold still." As many times as she'd had her leash clipped to her collar, Tasy still exuberantly wagged her tail and the rest of her body, making it tough for Dee to attach the braided tether. "Got it, you little rascal," Dee said. She nuzzled Tasy's neck affectionately then opened the car door.

The eager pooch leading the way, both friends began their run along the dirt road that rimmed the west side of the World Heritage Site. The rain had filled the holes in the uneven road creating a maze of puddles. Tasy splashed straight through while Dee jumped and maneuvered around them to avoid a muddy drenching.

They came to the end of the road and turned onto the footpath leading past the monument, Tasy tugged forward pulling with all her might. "Not so fast!" The leash jerked free from Dee's grasp. She stumbled. When she regained her balance, she saw the leash snaking through the air behind a vanishing blur of white. *She's heading for the security access gate! She must have seen a fox maybe a rabbit.*

Dee scanned the area. "Tasy, Tasy," Then louder, "TA-SY!"

Dee was sure the little dog would have come bounding back by now, tail between her legs, but there was no sign of her.

Then, "Arf, Arf, Arf, Arf"

She's holding something at bay! Sounds like digging! She can't be digging inside Stonehenge!

Tasy was not a thoroughbred anything. The people at the pet rescue center told Dee that her features and behavior identified the fox terrier in her. True to that heritage, she dug. She had to be closely watched in the garden, especially with the landlady' s beautifully tended flowers. Sarah took exception to Tasy, but not when it came to her perennials.

Dee began to run. The footpath was muddy and she slipped and fell on her knee. "Tasy, get back here right now!" She brushed off a clump of mud from the knee of her jeans.

"Arf, arf. Arf, arf, arf." Dee recognized Tasy's barking pattern—that little canine had found something. "I'm coming Tasy. Whatever it is, don't kill it."

The huge gate was her only option for quickly entering the secure area. Dee couldn't fit under the gate and the spikes along the top were nothing to challenge. As a member of Archaeology Assistants in Field Work for Bournemouth University, she hadn't yet earned her AABU tee shirt, but she'd earned the privilege of working Stonehenge. Now she wished she hadn't been so chatty when Professor Devans was opening the combination lock.

She stood staring at the little digits then decided to give it a try. She had a combination lock for her bike and when locking it she'd move only one disk out of order to make it easier to open the next time. *Maybe that's what Professor Devans did.* She studied the pattern of numbers. "That's it," Dee exclaimed. "Except for one digit, it's the number to the equipment store!"

Dee pulled hard and the gate's metal bar slid toward her. She stopped the heavy gate from fully opening, slid her slender body through the space and stepped inside the grounds of Stonehenge. Dee hurriedly pulled the gate closed then slid the bar back into its sheath. The lock went into her pocket as she took off to find Tasy.

Maybe she's chased a rabbit through the visitor's tunnel. Looking down the double-tiered ramp that led to the tunnel, Dee called, "Tasy!" She heard faint barking sounds; first two barks followed by three of the same urgency. The muffled message was unmistakable: Tasy's found something. Then Dee realized, *she's not near the tunnel.*

Turning in the direction of the stones, the anxious student scanned the landscape as she jogged toward the monument. Again, the pattern of barks repeated: two yips and then three. They sounded closer but not in the direction she was heading.

Dee turned toward the Heel Stone. It was a large uneven stone set off from the others, close to the road. She picked up her pace, then ran. A mound of freshly dug earth was growing larger at the base of the legendary boulder. She reached the site and saw Tasy submerged in a wide hole, Her white fur and black spots were an icky mess of matted earth.

"So this is where you are you naught—. What's this? Tas, what are you digging up?"

Dee fell down on her knees and lifted Tasy out of the hole and removed the soggy leash. She put the pup down and peered into the hole. The top edge and sides of an urn were visible as it sat upright in the earth. The urn's opening was packed to the top with what appeared to be more of the same earth into which it had been placed.

"No handles. It has no handles. You found a collared urn!" Dee took Tasy's head between both of her grimy hands and looked straight into her pup's inquisitive eyes. "You're some terrier, but I don't get it, Tas, why dig here?"

She'd solve that mystery later. Now she needed advice. "Professor Devans will know what to do." She pointed at Tasy. "You stay here."

Dee held her opened hand as a command signal. "Stay," The well-trained canine knew just what to do. She lay down with her head held alert and ears pointed up. Her forepaws rested at the edge of the hole.

"That's a good girl. I'll be right back."

Her mind raced as she ran to the car. *This has got to be a hoax. Someone must have planted it; maybe put a dead mouse on top of where he buried the pottery. He had to find a fake urn and fill it with debris, dig a hole without being seen, put everything back and hope someone's dog would find it and make a big deal in the press. He's probably waiting for tomorrow's headlines,* "Dog Uncovers Valuable Artifact at Stonehenge." *I've got to call Prof!*

By now, the clouds had hidden the last of the sun. None of this mattered to the archaeology student. Dee felt the rain brush her face as she skidded on the mud in front of her 'Pug,' what Dee called her Peugeot 309. She had to make a fast decision: Dirty clothes? Or dirty mobile keypad? She wiped the mud from her hands on her sweatshirt. Idly she thought, *What could be better than Heritage mud to stain my BU sweatshirt?*

She opened the door and reached into her knapsack pulling out the pay-as-you-go mobile. She searched the directory for Professor Devans' number and hit the call button. She waited; it seemed forever before he picked up.

"Devans here."

"Professor Devans, this is Dee.."

"Your credit is running low," came an automated message.

"Please don't lea …"

Be be be be be be …

"Damn! What good is this thing?" Dee threw the phone onto the passenger seat, slammed the door, started the engine and drove to the security gate. She got out and opened the back door, unbuckled Tasy's bed and wedged it on the floor behind the front seat.

With the passenger door open she went to the 309's boot, opened it and removed the oilcloth liner. She grabbed her Archaeologist's Kit and leaving the boot's door up and the gate ajar, trudged off to the Heel Stone.

With gloved hands and brushes and sometimes a trowel, she worked carefully around the artifact. Tasy, wet but cleaner from the intermittent rain, wagged her tail as she looked on.

Finally, Dee stood up and brushed strands of wet hair from her forehead. She'd managed to free the vessel from the earth in one piece. It stood before her in all its muddy magnificence like a mirage in the dusk of day.

There was no time to contemplate its story.

She got back to work and covered the empty hole with the oilcloth weighing it down along the edges with sodden earth, hoping that would prevent further damage to the original burial spot.

The archaeology student knew she shouldn't be doing this herself. Measurements, photographs, and earth samples should be taken at every stage of removal. She also knew that thieves could be found at night chipping away at the stones. Any article—fake or authentic—would not be safe while unattended at that remote site.

It was getting dark and a cool breeze made her shiver. *What about filling out the required Standard Finds Recording Form?* she wondered. *This isn't a farmer's field or someone's back yard. This is Stonehenge ... a World Heritage Site ... how many laws have I broken?*

Dee wrapped Tasy's leash around the artifact hoping it would reinforce and protect the urn while she carried it to the Pug. Snapping her tool kit shut, she shouldered its strap and gingerly picked up the urn. "Wow, this thing's heavy. Let's go Tas."

With the gate ajar and the back door of her car open she had a clear path to the security of the bed. She placed the urn on its side and the fleece lining of Tasy's bed enveloped it.

Dee stood up and removed her dirty gloves. Studying her "new passenger," she thought, *this may be the trip of its life, even if it is in a Pug.*

Dee turned her sweatshirt inside out and shaped it into a nest on the front passenger seat. She knew Tasy would appreciate snuggling into her master's earthy scent during the road trip to BU.

In damp T-shirt and muddy jeans, the archaeology student set the Pug in motion, but her mind was on the story she would tell Professor Devans. Idly patting Tasy's head, her rapid heartbeat slowed to a steady pace.

It took forty-five minutes, the 309's best time, to reach BU's archaeology department, and by then it was dark. As she drove up to the equipment store, she wondered why the Brits couldn't just call the place they stored artifacts and paraphernalia a storeroom. The term had confused her when she first arrived as a student from Greece. Her thoughts now went to the present dilemma. She turned the engine off, but left the headlights on since the ground floor of the building was dark. She got out of the car and looked up, a light was on in one of the upstairs labs. Encouraged, she ran up and tried the door. Locked.

Cold, hungry, and desperate, she returned to her car and slumped onto the seat. A silhouette walking across the room upstairs caught her attention.

"Someone's upstairs! Tasy, hold your ears, I'm going to make a loud noise!"

The perceptive dog jumped across Dee's lap and out the Pug's open door, sensing her master's wishes. Dee leaned on the horn and blasted.

Be-e-e-e-e-p!

Tasy caught on. She ran back to the open car door and stood waiting for the next horn blast. After every blast of the horn, she barked three times. Finally, the loud commotion worked. Dee saw someone look out of the second-floor window, so she waved frantically, scooted out of the car, and motioned for help.

A light snapped on in the equipment store and Professor Devans appeared. When he walked toward her, his concerned expression relieved her pent-up tension. Tears prickled the corner of her eyes. She wiped them away leaving muddy smudges on her face.

By the looks of his normally bright and tidy student, Geoffrey Devans knew he had correctly interpreted the dropped call.

"What is it, Dee? Come in. You look like you could use a cup of coffee and some dry things." He motioned for her to proceed through the door. "I thought you might be in trouble when we lost contact on the phone a while ago."

Tasy barked.

The professor opened the door wider. "You too. Come along."

The little pooch accepted the invitation and trotted in.

Dee shook her head. "There's something in my car you've got to see right now Professor Devans! It's on the floor in Tasy's seat."

"Right!" He let the door close behind him sensing this was no time to probe Dee with questions.

Dee led him to the back of the car and opened the passenger side door. "It's pretty heavy," she said, and bent over to pick it up.

"No, no, let me do that. Can you move the driver's seat forward? Looks like this thing's really wedged in here. I can't seem to get a grip on it."

"The seat won't go forward or backward. Sorry."

Professor Devans turned to look at Dee with an understanding expression. "OK, not a problem. Get the door for me."

He felt around until he found the mud-encrusted rim. Putting one arm underneath the dog's bed and the other one around the object, Professor Devans maneuvered it out from behind the driver's seat. As he carried it through the door, he looked at Dee and said, "I know you're bursting to tell me what this is all about. But, you know the procedure; you can't tell me anything yet. Now I get to practice what I preach!"

"Right! You have ten minutes. I'll not prejudice you," she said, proudly playing the role of professor.

Professor Devans' reputation for following his prescribed procedure was well known: When first identifying a relic, he required his students to gather all observable evidence before asking questions. The professor didn't want someone else's statements to prejudice the student's initial observation.

Not a word was spoken as the artifact made its way to the lift. Tasy returned just in time to join the solemn procession as the elevator door closed and all three were whisked to the second floor.

Devans set the heavy load on the surface of a laboratory table. He wiped his forehead.

Dee was shivering.

"First things first," Devans said. "Let's get you a lab coat. You must be freezing." He grabbed a white coat from its hook and handed it to Dee. "Relax a moment." He pulled out his office chair and motioned for her to sit down. "Catch your breath. We could all do for some nourishment. I'll call in an order at Costa. My treat. What can I get you?"

"I'm too excited; I don't think I can eat." Dee wrapped her arms around herself to stop shivering. "On second thought, I'll take a cafe latte, if you don't mind."

"My pleasure." He phoned in an order, and then searched for a makeshift water bowl for the dog. Filling an empty Costa cup, Professor Devans set it beside the thankful terrier.

Dee smiled her thanks.

The professor pulled up a chair close to the object in the dog's bed. He swung the chair around backwards and sat down facing the find. Studying it, he took mental notes.

Dee looked at the clock on the wall. "You've got three minutes left, Professor Devans."

The sound of footsteps in the hall interrupted him. "That was quick." He got up to pay the coffee bar attendant, then returned with a tray of food. "I got you a ham and cheese," he said, setting the tray on an empty table. "Don't feel like you have to eat it now. You can pack it up for later, if you like."

Dee pulled her stool closer to the food, picked up her latte, and scooped up the sandwich. Professor Devans set down a paper plate for Tasy with most of a tuna fish sandwich on it. Dee eyed the large portion and looked back at her professor.

"My stomach doesn't do well when I'm this excited," he said, taking a deep breath. "Dee, you've found something that appears to be authentic … quite interesting! Of course, we'll have to test it, but a collared urn like this could very well be from an early Bronze Age culture. My observation, however, gives me the impression that the firing process was exceptional. There are few visible cracks. It has a simple ornamental design. That may mean it was crafted for the common burial or everyday use as a storage vessel." He paused. "Now, your turn, Dee. How in the world did you find it?"

Like the repeating rounds of an automatic weapon, Dee's words fired from her mouth. "Tasy and I were jogging around the site. All of a sudden she pulled so hard on her leash it slipped out of my hand. It must have been a baby fox or maybe a rabbit. I didn't see it. She ran away before I could reach her, she'd dug this huge hole. It was so deep I had to get down on my knees to lift her out. That's when I saw it. It's probably a hoax or something. I'm thinking someone put it in the ground and is waiting to see the morning headlines: DOG DIGS UP RARE ARTIFACT AT BASE OF HEEL STONE; Professor Devans I couldn't get the mes …"

"Heel Stone?" His eyes widened. The hand holding his cup of coffee began to shake. Coffee sloshed onto the table as he set it down. He peered around the lab double-checking to make sure no one else was there. Beads of perspiration appeared at his hairline. He leaned toward Dee and whispered, "You can't be talking about Stonehenge, can you?"

"Well, yeah," she replied sheepishly.

The professor lowered his head into both his hands. "The hell with coffee, I need a gin and tonic!"

"I'm really sorry, Professor Devans, but I couldn't leave it there." She mopped up the spilled coffee with her lab coat sleeve. "I'll do whatever you—"

He waved her off. "We'll figure this out, but not here."

His mind raced.

Finally, he burst out, "I've got to leave word with authorities, but which one?" He abruptly changed plans. "I'm going to the site now. It's got to be official. Want to help? You'll get a first-hand lesson on proper procedure, especially when you have the right gear." He got up to leave.

"Yes, yes, Oh, yes! Come on Tasy!"

Professor Devans stopped just inches from the door. "That lab coat's not going to work outside." He hurried over to a stool and retrieved a student's forgotten sweatshirt. "Are you all right wearing this?" He handed Dee the borrowed warmth and she took it, knowing she'd only be too glad to return the favor.

Off they went to Stonehenge: Dee and Tasy in the Pug and Professor Devans in his red Spitfire.

Devans was first to arrive. He parked next to the security gate and noticed that the lock was missing. *How'd she get that lock open?* he thought, walking to the back of the Triumph. He gathered his equipment and waited. Soon, he heard Dee's car. "That engine could do for an overhaul," he murmured, waving assistance to Dee as she guided the 309 into the remaining small space.

He put on his miner's light and gave one to Dee. After she had adjusted it, he handed her the optical line meter survey kit to carry. He picked up the leveling staff, camera, and lights.

"We're ready," he said, and student and teacher hurried to the Heel Stone. Tasy bounded ahead.

"Holy sh—! Oops," Devans said. He was not by nature a profaniteur and he certainly didn't want Dee to believe otherwise, so he stopped in mid-curse and aimed his beam at the dog who stood beside him peering at her handiwork. "This is one huge hole, Tasy. Why'd you dig here? Did you smell something?" Of course, he didn't expect an answer; he was perplexed and thought the whole incident incredibly bizarre. *So why not talk to a dog?*

Tasy looked up at the professor and wagged her tail, and then finished with a friendly bark.

Dee saw the two in "conversation" as she approached. Her miner's light bobbed up and down with every labored step, and she was grateful to set down her load. Tasy trotted up to Dee, who gave her a friendly pat. "Whatever you asked Tasy, Professor Devans, she said 'Yes!'"

He smiled. "I'm not sure I believe her. How long had Tasy been missing before you reached this hole?"

"Well, it seemed like forever. First, I had to figure out the correct number sequence for the combination lock and then find Tasy. Oh, I don't know, maybe five, ten minutes." She stopped for a moment. "Hey, I remember something else, though. Her first barks were intruder alerts—you know, when a stranger approaches and the dog's surprised. Tasy makes continuously loud, sharp barks. She only did one string of those alerts, then the other barks told me she'd found something."

Shaking his head in disbelief that a pet dog would spontaneously customize a bark pattern like that, Devans went about attaching the spotlight to the tripod. He pressed the button and the ground around the hole lit up. "Now, that's more like it. See what I mean about having the right equipment?"

Dee wasn't listening. "Do you think there was someone, a person, here and Tasy scared him away?" Her eyes opened wide. "That's spooky!"

"Well, I don't know about dogs and how fast they dig, but this hole's a bit large!" he said, snapping photographs before handing the camera to Dee. "I want you to record a sequence of shots that show the earth as I scrape it from the outer edges of the hole. Look here, Dee, get this shot." Professor Devans pointed to marks in the earth he'd exposed.

"Got it," Dee said as she took several different angles of the marks. "Those look like shovel cuts," she volunteered. "They're pretty deep!"

"Good observation." The professor was pleased.

"You're right! Tasy couldn't have done that!" She handed Professor Devans the camera and reached for the tape. "Here, I'll measure it."

He put the camera strap around his neck and removed a notebook and pen from his pocket and jotted the measurements when Dee called out the numbers.

"Now, we ask the question was someone burying the urn or removing it? We'll let the analyses tell us."

Hours later, after they'd protected the site with a perimeter of bailing twine and metal pegs, they posted Keep Out signs, and headed to the gate. Dee caught up to her professor. "Professor Devans," she reached into her pocket, "here, I almost forgot I had this. Just call me Hou-DEE-ni. You know, spelled with two e's." She smiled and handed him a muddy combination lock.

"Thanks. How'd you get the combination?"

"You taught me to be a keen observer," she said, as she walked to the rear of her car and caught a glimpse of his smile.

He packed up his gear and locked the security gate. "See you tomorrow. Cleaning and documenting shouldn't take too long.

I'll meet you at the equipment store entrance. Don't blast the horn, either. I already know it's the one thing on that Pug of yours that really works." He smiled at his own joke.

Dee was too exhausted to think of a good retort. In the early dawn, she saw Tasy's ears perk up. "Is Tasy invited too?"

"OK, sure, bring Tasy. She started this adventure. I guess it's her right," he conceded.

"Thank you, Professor Devans. Did you hear that, Tasy? It's an adventure and you started it."

Master and dog hopped into the 309 for what was left of the night.

Professor Devans headed home to a gin and tonic.

Part 2

Shortly before noon the next day, the Pug rolled into the unloading zone at the equipment store. Dee and Tasy were raring to go.

"Looks like you've both made up for the lost sleep last night." Professor Devans ushered in his student and her dog and they proceeded to the lab. "By the way, we're going to have some help with the analyses. I've asked Lisbet Fleming to perform her magic."

Devans handed Dee her tools and gloves. "Hey, Tasy." He bent down and petted her head. She responded by wagging her tail. "Sorry I don't have any tools for you, but I've got some dog biscuits."

Tasy barked twice, and this time her whole backside and tail wagged.

"No barking Tasy. We're in a quiet zone." Dee held out her hand, fingers closed, and waved it back and forth. Tasy sat down and waited. "OK, come …"

"Smart dog! Wish that technique worked on my students," the surprised professor replied.

"Hi," Lisbet said cheerily as the three entered the second-floor characterization lab. She knelt down and patted Tasy. "So, I understand you're The Discovery Dog." Lisbet knew firsthand about grandkids and pets. Sometimes she wasn't sure which she preferred, but today Tasy was queen.

"I get to play with my babies today, Tasy. Isn't that great?"

Lisbet's "babies" in this case weren't the diaper-changing kind; instead, they were the machines that analyzed her samples with specific processes to determine their compositions.

"Dee, you probably didn't know, but my thermoluminescence instrument has been down for a month. It was finally repaired Friday, so we'll be able to date the samples. Glad this happened when it did. We'll get a head start and, anyway, I'm excited, it's not every day I get to analyze a find from Stonehenge!"

Through dedication, precision, and good instincts, Lisbet Fleming had attained her current position as chief analyst of antiquities at Bournemouth University. She also sat on the board of Great Britain's Heritage Trust, which added to her stature in the world of archaeology.

Volunteering time at work was not a problem for Lisbet if the request was from Professor Devans. His projects were always interesting, a welcomed relief from the tedium of her everyday analyses. She would never forget the time he had asked her to analyze a specimen of exploding toothpaste. The men's room had to be closed down so she could take a sample from the ceiling.

Now, Professor Devans spoke up, "I've assigned our Stonehenge Heel Stone artifact as 'TAS309.' Like the name?" He looked at Dee.

"Cool! Hear that, Tas? You've been immortalized in archaeology literature." She scratched Tasy's head.

"Lisbet, not to keep you in the dark, Dee drove the artifact here in her Peugeot 309. I thought the Pug deserved its rightful recognition. I found no conflict when I skimmed the ID database. Dee, do a full backup check on the identification tomorrow." The professor was eager to begin. "Let's get started. I'll take a video of the initial removal. Then we'll rotate jobs. We should be finished in no time."

Devans handed a trowel to Dee and the logbook to Lisbet. Dee carefully scraped away the moist top layer of earth, putting each portion into a receptacle on the table. Below that she found the earth dry and hard. She continued slowly while Lisbet took notes. With earthen samples removed, packaged, and labeled, the project proceeded. Professor Devans completed the video and then assisted Dee.

"What's this? Seeds!" Dee tipped her trowel and let the three seeds mixed with dry earth roll into the tray. Lisbet picked up the camera and took a few photographs.

Devans leaned his head into the jar. "There's more where that came from, lots more," he said as he tipped the urn and poured more into the tray. They resembled hardened, wrinkled peas. He looked deep into the cavity beyond the collar. "It's full of seeds … could this be a storage jar for seeds? That's strange." He set his trowel down, removed his gloves, and walked over to a wall of shelves filled with reference material.

"I know I've seen those seeds before. They're from the legume family." He pulled out volume *L* of the *Encyclopedia of Plants and Flowers*. "Here it is: *Lathyrus cicera*." He read aloud, "*Lathyrus cicera* is a species of wild pea. It says it's native to Europe, the Middle East, and North Africa." He turned the page and remarked, "Right on! The images look similar. Whatever you do, don't ingest these little devils. This is a quote: 'If eaten in large quantities, can cause neurolathryrism.'" He added, "Keep Tasy away. Even though they appear to be degraded, those seeds could cause spastic paralysis and pain."

"I've hit something solid. I need help!" Dee said.

Professor Devans put his gloves back on and picked up his trowel. "Let me have a try at this." He lifted out more seeds and exposed some fabric. He put the trowel down and felt with his hands. It seemed that several layers of wrapping were protecting a hard flat object. "Let's get a video of this. Dee, take the camera and wait until Lisbet and I get the object free. I'll tell you when."

Devans and Lisbet cleared away more of the seeds. "OK, shoot," the professor said.

Perched on a chair, Dee was able to center the camera's viewfinder on the object as it was removed.

"Careful, the fabric." Devans guided Lisbet further. "Ease it down. Excellent. Don't touch a thing!"

Silence.

No one in the lab had talent for weaving, but instinctively they recognized a fabric woven by the hands of a master.

"This must have once been a cherished possession," Professor Devans surmised.

"Look at those tiny stitches," Dee said. "They actually depict swimming fish. Wow!"

Lisbet leaned down closer to examine the workmanship.

"Could you please record a description of the fabric?" Devans said. The request broke the silence and jolted both women back to reality.

Lisbet removed her gloves. "Sure," she said, sitting down at her laptop.

Dee was curious. "How did they make red?" Though faded, the red hue of the fibers was unmistakable.

"We know that ivy gum or resin from *Hedera helix* has been used to make red as early as the Bronze Age." Professor Devans continued, "It's a vine … clings to almost anything. Maybe that's it. don't really know yet." Then he picked up two pairs of tongs and delicately unwrapped the cloth. "Get this on video, Dee."

Lisbet typed: *Tightly woven fabric of unknown origin incorporating images of swimming fish. Color is faded red.*

Devans gingerly unfolded the fragile fabric. He didn't dare flatten it out. Carefully the ends of the fabric were pulled away and a curious object emerged. "Lock the door, Dee." The professor's receding hairline glistened with perspiration. "Let's keep the details between us until we have some accurate findings. I had a call early this morning asking about what's been found at Stonehenge. The last thing we want is the press publishing rumors."

He looked up while still holding the tongs in position. "Listen carefully, you two." Dee walked back to the table and Lisbet lifted her hands from the keyboard. "Once this discovery becomes news, you're going to be interviewed and quoted. Your name may appear in the literature—Lisbet, I know you're used to this—but Dee, you've got to be sure you approve every one of your quotes before the media release it. Remember, our research is *inconclusive* at this time."

"Wow, you really think this could go global?" Dee's eyes widened with excitement.

"I didn't say 'global.' That's your word." Professor Devans smiled. "Lisbet, please put your gloves back on. I want you to pull away the leather edging. It appears to be protecting the jagged edge of a small plate or bowl that's been broken in half." He put the tongs down and pointed.

Dee instinctively picked up the camera and turned on the video.

Using the fingers of both hands, Lisbet slowly freed the crescent-shaped object from its leather sheath. A sparkling brilliance emanated from the semicircular artifact.

Dee momentarily forgot her job and the video camera suddenly began to record the lab table. She almost dropped the camera. "Wow! What is that?" she said, regaining her composure.

"Dee, stay focused. Take this down, Lisbet." Professor Devans' heart started racing and his no-nonsense attitude kicked in.

Lisbet poised her shaking hands on the keyboard. "Ready, Professor Devans."

Still holding the tongs in position, Professor Devans dictated, "We have a crescent-shaped, brilliantly glittering, small plate-like object. Its raised lip is rimmed with a gold band; it seems to be a perfect arc. It appears to have been broken through the center leaving a sharp, jagged edge. There's a partial inscription. The decorative features include . . ."

The detailed description took several minutes. Measurements were taken and recorded.

Professor Devans looked at Lisbet. "Looks like I've got a bigger project for you than I thought. Hope you can handle this. I need the composition of the urn and the plate. On the plate, you need to analyze the gold rim, the black script, the red ring, and the black substance of the letters *I* and *Zed*."

Lisbet nodded. "I can do that. What about the shiny coating? I'll analyze that too," she volunteered. "We can do most of the analyses here." Devans continued. "I'll ship samples of the cloth, seeds, and leather to Ellen at Irvine, express DHL. She's got the quickest turn-around for carbon dating results. If she's free tomorrow, she'll expedite it immediately as a favor to me. Even so, she's expensive. We could save a lot if we had our own instrument." Then his enthusiasm wavered. "Think what a waste of time and money this will be if this turns out to be someone's idea of a joke! Dee, maybe your hoax theory has some merit. I don't understand how these artifacts can be connected." Professor Devans stepped back and looked pensively at the artifacts. "The urn looks like it was made in the early Bronze Age. The plate or bowl; well, I've never seen anything like it from craftsmen of that era. It's much too sophisticated for their four-thousand-year-old technology. It looks like it held something small, but what? The symbols on its rim could be a script or simple logogram with a message of some kind."

Devans paused and rubbed his chin, "The more I try to reason this out, the more it seems like a prank. Possibly someone planting it was surprised by a Tasy attack." He turned and looked at Lisbet. "We'll know soon enough if we should involve the police."

She raised her eyebrows. "The police! I'll get right on this."

Dee felt Tasy scratching at her ankle. She looked down and saw a familiar look. "Of course, you're thirsty." She scrounged through the trash and found an empty paper Costa cup. As she rinsed it under the faucet, she glanced at the slogan: *What's That Smell?* Dee thought, *Smell! What was that smell?* "That's it, Tasy smelled something! Professor, she's too disciplined to bolt away from me; there must have been an odor that alarmed her for her to run off like that."

"Like Pot?" Lisbet joked.

"Well, now that you mention it, some type of smoking chemical might do it," Dee nodded.

"Hold that thought. We've got lab work and documentation to complete." Professor Devans took a key from his pocket.

"I can fill out the Standard Finds Recording Form," Dee volunteered.

He unlocked the file drawer that held the blank forms used to record archaeological finds attributed to BU. "For now, let's just report the urn. Oh, I almost forgot the Conservation Form. Fill out what you can. I'll do the rest later." He handed Dee the forms then wiped his brow with the back of his hand. Pulling out a chair, Professor Devans sat backward on the seat. He thought better when he could lean on his arms, and there he sat, chin in hands, pondering well into the evening.

Part 3

Monday arrived. Professor Devans' students were ready for their first class of the day; it was his Archaeology Honors Program. They seemed unusually attentive as the professor addressed them.

"Unless you've been unconscious for the last forty-eight hours, you've heard about a find at Stonehenge. If you've been properly informed, you know the artifact ended up in BU's Archaeology Department. And if your informant was in this building, you know I haven't had much sleep. You may not know, however, that I'm running on adrenalin and can't wait to tell you the story." He paused a long moment then resumed, "after today's test."

A unanimous groan emanated from the students.

"Oh, and don't rush through the test. I need time to drink my coffee." Chatter escalated as it buzzed through the large, sunny classroom. While a volunteer passed out the tests, Professor Devans swung his chair around backward and sat down. Then he picked up his coffee, took a sip, and leaned his chin on his folded arms.

He thought about the astute observations and exciting hypotheses he could draw from his students' supple minds, if they knew the whole story. The notion gave him a warm inner glow. He'd sworn Dee and Lisbet to secrecy concerning the contents of the urn; so none of that discovery would be known outside the circle of three. For now, he would make the *empty* urn's discovery an exciting lesson for these students.

"So, you made this a one-cup test," he said, swallowing the last drop of coffee. He put the empty cup down, got up and reversed his chair, and stacked the completed tests in a neat pile. He cleared his throat. "*Ahem*, well, are we ready to discuss TAS309? As my honors' class you have the distinction of being."

Ring, ring! The phone on his desk interrupted his lecture. Since he only accepted emergency calls during class time, he wondered, *who could it be*? "Excuse me, this must be important." He walked to his desk and picked up the phone. "Devans here."

"Sorry to disturb your class, Professor." It was Lisbet. "Something's not right with the data. I need you to see this before I go any further with the analyses."

"I'll be right down, Lisbet." He sensed the emergency in her voice. Retrieving a binder from his desk drawer, the professor realized that the students had opened their textbooks. "No need to stay here. I've got to solve a problem that may take a while. See you on Thursday," he said, dismissing the class. "Oh, and brush up on collared urns." He gave them a thumbs-up and hurried out the door.

A little winded, Devans arrived at the ground-floor lab and peered through the small pane of glass. Lisbet saw him and unlocked the door.

"What's up?" he asked.

"I ran identical samples several times … you've got to see these TLD results!" Lisbet checked to make sure the door was locked. She handed him the printouts.

He scanned the paper. "This is impossible it *can't* be!" Devans reached out with his other hand to steady the shaking document and the binder under his arm fell to the floor. "Let me see your calibration standards results." They both ignored the fallen notebook.

Lisbet pulled out a chair. "Why don't you have a seat? I've got the calibration results right here." She handed him the document.

"*Hmm*, these calibrations are precise and you've got a perfect match on both runs for each artifact. Do you have the bulk and trace metal results?"

"That's the other problem." She picked up the spreadsheet.

"You read. I'll listen," he said. Lisbet rattled off the facts, "The plate's composition is zirconia with 3 percent yittria, and its outer band is made of 24-karat gold. The plate's inner ring is ruby. The black letters and figures are composed of multiwalled carbon nanotubes. The entire surface is coated with a diamond film." She finished and looked up.

"If my geo-chem course served me right, the melting point of zirconia is 2,715 degrees centigrade. People from the Bronze Age could produce heat up to 1,300 degrees centigrade, but never over two thousand!" Professor Devans was perspiring. He unbuttoned his cardigan and loosened the collar of his shirt. "Why is it so blasted hot in here?"

"I'll get you some water." Lisbet filed her document and headed for the door.

The room was spinning. Professor Devans got up to open a window.

Lisbet heard a thud and rushed back to see him sprawled on the floor. Before she had time to call for emergency assistance, he was up on his knees.

"Don't bother to call for help," he said. "I'm fine. I just tripped on that bloody binder." He dismissed the fall with a wave of his hand. "Let's find Dee. Try the library, OK? The DHL package from Irvine should be here … I'll check on that. We need to connect the dots. Meet me in the osteology lab. It's much cooler there."

"Are you sure you're OK?"

He picked up the notebook from the floor and went to the file cabinet drawer where Lisbet put the spreadsheet.

"I'm fine! Just wasn't paying attention. I'm going to make a copy of these analyses." He took the sheet out of the drawer and put it in the pocket of the binder.

Lisbet locked up the lab on her way out behind Devans.

Part 4

Cool air wafted through the osteology lab's window. It felt refreshing and Devans inhaled deeply. Setting his water bottle on a table, he opened the DHL express envelope. Inside, there was a brief personal greeting from Ellen including a thank-you for his request. He ignored the invoice and placed it back in the folder. The lab results were on a separate sheet. He scanned those until he came to the concluding results:

RC dating of Lathyrus cicera seeds using AMS method: age 3600 ± 36 BP
RC dating of Woven Nettle Cloth using AMS method: age 3600 ± 36 BP
RC dating of Leather Sheath using AMS method: age 3600 ± 36 BP

A loud knock startled him back to reality. He unlocked the door; it was Lisbet and Dee. Dee bustled in carrying a tray of coffee. "It's my turn to treat," she said, her cheerful voice filling the air.

"That's right thoughtful of you, I can sure use some," Devans said, grabbing one.

Lisbet dropped a file folder on the table. "I didn't have a chance to review the results of the soil analyses with you. They're all here." Drawing up two stools, she arranged them close to Devans' straight-backed chair.

They all sat down and got comfortable.

Devans muttered, "I'd forgotten about the soil tests." He interlaced his fingers behind his head and rocked gently back and forth. Abruptly he stopped rocking. "Let me guess, Lisbet. The soil inside and under the lip of the urn have the same trace metal distribution ratio, but the soil sample from the undisturbed area surrounding the hole has a different distribution."

"You've almost got it," Lisbet said, nodding her head. "It's just that the soil sample from the undisturbed area is *significantly* different."

"Good, that means the urn has been buried there since the Bronze Age! Let's reevaluate our data so far. Dee, write this reminder on the top of the board, please."

She scooted her stool back and walked to the blackboard. Chalk in hand, she waited for the professor to continue.

"BP equals Before Present. Since the standard archaeological present is 1950, 3600 BP is interpreted as 1650 BCE, or Before Common Era." Then he gathered up his notes, Lisbet's results, and Ellen's carbon-dating information and compiled a list of analytical findings and extraneous facts. As he stated each bit of information, Dee transcribed it on the board. By the time he finished, she had filled it to the bottom.

Satisfied with the raw data, Devans pointed to the board on the adjacent wall. "Write 'Conclusion' on that one, so we can summarize everything."

They agreed each person should write his or her personal conclusions privately. After five minutes, Devans handed Lisbet his and Dee's paper. "OK, you're good at consensus," he said. Then he turned to Dee, "We'll give Lisbet some time to identify the common conclusions and then I'd like you to write everything on the board."

Lisbet studied all three papers. "This isn't as hard as I thought it would be. Here's our consensus." She read each point slowly to give Dee time to record the information. "One, the urn and the plate were removed from earth that had been undisturbed for more than three thousand years. Two, carbon-dating results indicate the artifacts are older than three thousand years. Three, there's no evidence that the technology from the Bronze Age could have produced the plate. Four, the plate appears to be broken in half. Five, the script or logogram on the plate is unknown, and six, Tasy was not the only one digging at the base of the Heel Stone. The final consensus: This is *not a hoax*," she concluded, dropping the pages on the table.

Devans rubbed his chin. "I'm hoping to find someone to decipher the script or logogram on the plate," he said. "I spent yesterday evening searching the Internet for experts who may be able to interpret symbols that resemble early Greek hieroglyphic script. I discovered that Professor Emmett L. Bennett, now retired from the University of Wisconsin, is the preeminent scholar on Linear B Script. Problem is, he's retired and we'd have to get approval from the budget committee to contact him. Then, his fees would probably be astronomical—"

"Wait," Dee interrupted, "I know someone; you won't believe it." She was so excited she jumped off her stool. Leaning toward Professor Devans, she continued, "My grandfather! He lives in Santorini, you know, it's a little Greek Island. He's just the greatest guy. Please listen. He's met Professor Bennett, in fact, they're friends." She explained, "My grandfather's a member of the Archaeological Society of Athens. He studies Linear B and has been working to decipher Linear A. Gramps told me about the time he was in Athens when Professor Bennett received The Gold Cross of the Order of Honor. That's the highest award the Greek government can bestow on anyone—. At least that's what Gramps told me. Gramps has pictures and everything. I've seen them. I'll call him. He'll really be excited to help! You've gotta meet Gramps! At least he can tell us if it's Linear A or B script."

Professor Devans sensed the sincerity in Dee's offer, but he couldn't hand over an artifact of such potential value to a student's grandfather he'd never met. "I don't know, Dee," Devans said, "Greece isn't down the motorway. I'll have to think about it. Now that we've got all the test results, there are more forms to fill out. I can use your help with that." He was trying to change the subject, but inwardly he was tantalized by Dee's proposal.

Lisbet sensed Devans' quandary. "You know, you and Dee could take three emergency days off. Dee, your grandfather's really ill, and, Geoffrey, you were called to the University for your vote as an honorary councilor of the Archaeological Society of Athens. That's all I know. I don't remember any of the rest of this conversation.

"I'll book your flights, Professor, and bill it as a professional expense. You can answer questions later. Think about it while I check the airlines' schedules. That OK with you?"

The good professor was not paying attention to Lisbet's I'm-taking-over attitude. He was planning to research Dee's grandfather. "What's his full name, Dee?"

"It's Aristotle Maritimis. Oh, everyone on Santorini knows him—they call him Sailor Cum Laude. He gets a kick out of that."

Dee was excited by the possibility of visiting her grandfather. "Lisbet, when you make our travel arrangements, make sure we arrive in the morning. He likes working early in the day; he retired from afternoons long ago. If you want to hear his stories, then afternoons are great. Oh, I can't wait!" She threw her arms around Lisbet. "I'll bring you back a volcanic necklace—they polish it up, you know." By now, Dee was convinced they would be going. "You won't be sorry, Professor Devans," she sang out.

"Wait a minute," he said. "I still have to think about it. This may be a bad idea … I just don't know." He paused for several moments. "When's your last class today, Dee?"

"I have a three o'clock elective with Dr. Wright. You know, it's her 'Fashion Through the Ages Seminar.' She won't miss me—there're more than two hundred students in that class."

"Check in with me at four. One way or another, I'll have a decision."

"OK, sure, I'll calm down. You'll see." She checked her enthusiasm. "I guarantee you won't be disappointed in Gramps."

"Lisbet, check into flights, I need to register my vote in person as an honorary councilor of the Archaeological Society of Athens, they'll accept that as a professional expense. Now, I've got some research of my own to do."

Lisbet rolled her eyes and smiled at Dee. "If I weren't so tied down with grandkids, I'd get on that plane with you two. I have a feeling this is going to be another ET adventure!"

"ET" was Lisbet's expression that meant beyond peculiar. It was her way of preserving the memory of Professor Devans' Exploding Toothpaste study.

"Glad to be one of your secret agents," Lisbet said, just before she left to book their flights.

***

Lisbet, Dee, Professor Devans, and Tasy were on their way to Heathrow Airport. Lisbet had managed to book a direct flight for two that evening to Athens, Greece. She couldn't remember ever organizing a trip so quickly; she even managed to fill the tank before loading everyone into her car.

They had been traveling for an hour and twenty-five minutes, and Professor Devans rattled on about what Lisbet should say concerning their absence. "And don't forget Dee's urgency to fly to Santorini is strictly personal."

Lisbet turned off at the exit marked Departures. She decided to change the subject. "Dee, that leather bag of yours is darling."

Dee remarked, "Oh, I picked it up at a boot sale last year. I fell in love with the leather tooling, but it's a little too big to carry around campus. I'm glad it came in handy now; it's just the right size for the plate and the extra cushioning to protect it. No one will ever suspect we're transporting a valuable artifact."

"It goes under the seat in front of me, and it's not going to leave my sight," Devans said.

Lisbet could not resist the gibe. "You're going to look real *cute* entering the men's room with that adorable bag."

Before the professor could retort, they were in front of the departure gate of Aegean Airlines.

"Here we are," Lisbet said, pulling up to the curb.

Dee nuzzled her pet. "Tas, you be good for Lisbet. Promise?"

"I can't thank you enough," Devans said to Lisbet. "I'll call you tomorrow. Come on, Dee, we've got to hurry." Apparently he was not interested in long good-byes. He stood outside the car with their carry-on bags, clearly impatient to get to the gate.

"You two run along," Lisbet said, waggling her fingers good-bye. "Tasy and I will get on splendidly. Toodles."

As she pulled away from the curb, Lisbet's mind filled with nagging details. She worried if they would make the connecting flight from Athens to Santorini. Then she fretted about Devans' decision to have Dee tell her grandfather the whole story. To top off that worry, he had agreed to Aristotle's proposal to have an Archaeology PhD candidate from the United States join them.

Sometimes Professor Geoffrey Devans was a little too trusting, she thought.

Chapter 4
THE BLOOD

Part 1

The year is 2000 CE. Thorf Serendopolis, an archaeology graduate student, has unlocked the door of a secured records office at the Rosaland Franklin Institute of Genetics, RFI, in Titusville, New Jersey.

He had to hurry.

With perspiration beading on his forehead, Thorf Serendopolis set the dummy file on the desk and turned toward the wall that held rows of RFI patients' files. He scanned the S's:

Samuel, Scarlos, Schraft, Schultz, Seraf ... Serendopolis, there it is!

Using gloved hands, he slipped out the thick, heavy file and replaced it with the equally heavy counterpart. Then he unclipped and folded page two of the original document. Opening his medical coat, he slid the folded page deep into his pants' pocket.

With the original file wedged under his arm, he closed and locked the door to the private records office.

Treading softly through the outer office, he turned the knob and pushed open the door. Glancing left, then right, he was glad the hallway was empty. He peeled off the neoprene gloves, stuffed them in his coat pocket, and eased himself into the hall. He felt a sense of relief as he took a right turn in the corridor and passed a physician in a hurry, oblivious to his presence.

Young Serendopolis looked every bit the part of the clinical geneticist he was impersonating.

As he passed through the lobby, he smiled and nodded a greeting to the receptionist, then exited the renowned RFI.

There was no going back. The young man had stolen a comprehensive file that proved his DNA contained strange alleles. Why he was denied this information was still a mystery to him.

Thorf decided to drive the long way home across the narrow Thunder Bridge. His clammy hands slipped on the steering wheel as he guided the car over the noisy, rickety boards. Gripping the wheel harder, he turned left off the bridge onto Jacob's Creek Road. A drop of sweat stung his eyes as he drew an arm across his forehead. Then he glanced at the stolen file lying on the passenger seat.

I'll have to find a good hiding spot, he reasoned. *At least I've got what I need for now.*

Thorf checked his rearview mirror. *No one's behind me.* He relaxed his grip on the wheel and eased up on the gas. Driving along the winding country road, he thought about what happened the day before.

***

He had been summoned again to RFI. A team of genetic specialists wanted to draw more blood samples. *Why do they want more of my blood?* he thought, *I'm just an average kid.*

Well, maybe not a kid anymore—he had recently graduated from Princeton and was about to embark on a study program in Greece. All he wanted were the recommended inoculations for traveling abroad, and now this eager interest in his blood threatened to delay his flight.

He remembered how he burst out in anger at the medical team. "Why do I have to take more tests? I'm healthy. This is nuts. I just want to get vaccinated." Then he became suspicious.

"What are you hiding? Why won't you let me see my own test results?" He stared angrily at the stunned medical professionals. "You're just trying to patronize me!"

The offended student turned around and walked out, slamming the door.

It wasn't like him to slam a door. Five days ago, what should have been a routine doctor's visit had turned out to be a 'kidnapping by some lab rats,' as far as Thorf was concerned. All they wanted was his blood, more and more of it.

Why won't they just leave me alone?

He headed straight through the corridor to Reception—not bothering to acknowledge the receptionist, as was his custom—and out the door to the parking lot.

"Mr. Serendopolis!"

Thorf heard his name called out as he put the key in the lock of his Ford Escort. He turned to see Dr. Vishwa Balasubramanium, one of the consultants on the blood analysis team, walking briskly toward him. Thorf remembered him as the geneticist whose nametag had a piece of tape hiding the 'subramanium' part. The geneticist attempted to shorten his long name, but the tape kept falling off.

"Mr. Serendopolis, a moment of your time, please."

Vishwa, his short legs struggling to carry the weight of his rotund upper body, managed to reach Thorf before he opened the Escort's door. Thorf nodded his approval, curious to know the message that created such a flush in the doctor's face. He leaned against the car and folded his arms across his chest waiting for the doctor to catch his breath.

"I understand your anger, Mr. Serendopolis." Vishwa paused every now and then gasping for air. "What you've not been told is that none of our tests have found a match for your blood type. We've listed it as ABX. We didn't tell you because we'd like more of your blood to replicate the findings." He hesitated and checked his surroundings. Satisfied that no one was in earshot, Vishwa continued.

"That's not the only problem. We've just discovered some of your blood vials are missing. We don't know for sure, but we think they've been stolen."

Chest still heaving, the doctor—desperate to get his point across—added, "A young man like you, my God, you've got a perfectly pristine medical record. Think about it," he said, "according to your records you've never *even had* a cold." He shook his head. "There's something else. You possess exceptional skills in music and math, and you master any sport you try. There's not a university that wouldn't give you a graduate scholarship. That's far from the norm. We think your unique blood type may significantly contribute to your extraordinary abilities. If our tests prove accurate—and word gets out—there's no telling what someone would do to illegally obtain your blood."

Dr. Balasubramanium took a deep breath, and looking straight into the young man's eyes offered, "I can help you gain access to your files."

Part 2

Twenty hours after Thorf Serendopolis stole his medical records from RFI, *he's on a ship approaching the island of Santorini, Greece.*

Wind tossing his blond hair, Thorf stood a little taller than most of the passengers crowded on the open deck. He didn't appear to be a first-time visitor to this part of the world. On his back rested a wide-brimmed canvas hat hanging by its chin cord. The loose khaki shirt hid his broad shoulders and muscled biceps. His ankle-high cargo pants brushed the tops of his well-worn leather work boots.

It was no secret that archeology was this young man's passion. For passion beyond that, Thorf displayed no desire. To his female friends it was obvious that his good looks and smarts did not make up for the fact that his interests were single-minded. To them he appeared to have no idea that he was supposed to "like" them beyond their brain, much to their chagrin.

A student in one of Thorf 's university classes had confided to her friends, "Really, Thorf has no clue I like him. When I asked him if he'd like to meet for coffee he said, 'Sure, I don't have any time right now, but when I get back from Greece let's do that.' Then, you know what? His face turned really red and he said, 'I have an appointment. Thanks for the invite. See ya.' Then he walked away. Weird!"

Since his response to that invitation three days ago, Thorf hadn't given one thought to the incident.

The afternoon sun warmed his body as he scanned the eager-looking faces of the tourists shouldering their way to the railing. Everybody seemed unconcerned about his presence. Thorf relaxed his guard and found a spot at the rail, not to enjoy the scenery but to lean against the sturdy barrier.

He pulled from his pocket the now-familiar page two. According to Dr. Balasubramanium this was the summary of Thorf 's blood analysis. He glanced at it yet again. The heading displayed his name and other identifying information. In the center of the page, a graph illustrated the findings of the genetics team. Below the graph, a partial spreadsheet displayed numbers showing results of repeated blood tests.

Thorf hoped the fresh air would clear his thoughts so he could better wrap his mind around the meaning of this information.

He read it first using one hand to steady himself at the railing. The second time he perused it, he leaned his weight against the rail and used both hands to hold the page. Even that didn't help. No amount of repositioning himself or fresh air was going to help him interpret the data.

If some of the top geneticists in the world can't identify the alleles in my DNA, how can I expect to understand it? Thorf folded the document and slid it inside his pocket.

He looked behind him. Lots of people were aiming their cameras at the approaching land. *No need to be in their viewfinders,* he thought, as he turned his back toward them and gazed at the bustling seaport ahead.

Suddenly, Thorf felt light-headed. A burning sensation on the top of his head prodded him to put on his hat as he scrutinized the approaching cliffs.

A flash of familiarity to his surroundings swept over him. *I've been here before! No wait, I know I've never been here.* Unable to comprehend the deja vu, he tried to rationalize his feelings. *I've got an unmatchable blood type. Is it giving me delusions? Am I who I think I am? Now he couldn't suppress the painful memories of his past.*

Why me?

It's just another "why." *Why did my parents give me that exasperating name Thorf? Their answer never varied, "We like it," they'd say, and ignore my little boy protests about having to hear, "Thorf 's a dork, Thorf 's a dork," from those ignorant first graders who didn't even realize that "Thorf" and "dork" don't rhyme.*

Then his mind drifted aimlessly to another part of his past that ached for resolution.

Why Mexico? Why that particular archeological site where both of my parents' bodies were found? Why was I never given the details of their deaths? There'd been so many other sites they could've worked.

Shaking his head to clear his thoughts, Thorf decided not to dwell on his painful and mysterious past. The young archeology student straightened his back and scanned the blue sky. Taking a deep breath, he closed his eyes and ruminated about his upcoming independent study plans with Professor Maritimis.

Thorf was honored that the professor agreed to work with him, especially since his hypothesis piqued Maritimis's interest. Attending Santorini University while the professor was there was a lucky break for the young student. *He knows the sea, he knows the land, and he knows the people,* thought Thorf, *and someday, I hope to know it too.*

When he opened his eyes and looked up into the vast blueness surrounding him, Thorf remembered the sky was the same vibrant color the day his hypothesis had taken shape.

It had been three years ago. He was a Princeton sophomore then, and football season was in full swing. They were playing Cornell that particular day, if he remembered correctly. Thorf and his buddies, John, Roland, Sylvain, and Pete, had finished an archaeology seminar and were hungry for lunch. As they strolled to the student center for a sandwich, Pete mentioned, "Did you hear Thor Heyerdahl's on campus?" Although controversial in certain academic circles, Dr. Heyerdahl was a god among many archaeology students and he was Thorf 's idol!

"Let's find him," offered John.

The young men instantly agreed and soon they were standing in the entrance to the small cafeteria, eagerly scanning everybody's face.

Placing his hands on his hips to emphasize his solution, Sylvain said, "Come on guys, he would never be here. Let's try the Annex."

The Annex, a popular restaurant known for its inexpensive food and legendary customers, was across from the Firestone Library on Nassau Street.

The five of them headed to the below-ground entrance of the inconspicuous eatery. One behind the other, they bounded down the steps.

There they saw him, Thor Heyerdahl—hero, famous anthropologist, and master adventurer—was seated alone by the coat rack.

They laughed about it later, when Thorf, breathless with excitement, blurted out, "Sir, would you mind if we joined you for lunch?"

"Well, I'd be honored to join *you*," he said, surprised, but pleased to have the company. Standing up, the doctor motioned to a waiter to add a table.

Elbow to elbow, the six men began a most interesting afternoon.

Thorf never could remember what he ate, or even if he ate at all. He did recall the lively conversation and how infectious Thor Heyerdahl's passion was when regaling the young students with his adventures. They peppered him with questions about euro-centric theories of migration, the Ra, the *Ra II*, and, of course, the *Kon-Tiki.*

"You asked me why I burned the *Tigris.* Yes, it was a sacrifice. In her short life, the little reed boat helped us prove how the ancient Sumerians traveled so far and wide. With her death, she reawakened the world to the evils of war."

He paused, made a point to make eye contact with each young man, and then he continued, "You may someday find yourself having to demonstrate your contempt for evil without becoming evil in return. How you choose to demonstrate that contempt will determine the power of your message."

With those sobering thoughts, Thor Heyerdahl thanked the young men for enlivening his lunch and excused himself; he had an old friend to meet. After expressing their appreciation for giving them his time, everybody shook hands and said good-bye. *That chance meeting with Dr. Heyerdahl gave me the direction I needed,* Thorf recalled. From then on, Thorf knew the focus of his research. He would title his doctoral dissertation: "How Did Seemingly Distant and Unrelated Cultures of Antiquity Survive Natural Catastrophes to Co-mingle and Create Advanced Societies?"

A stiff breeze stung his eyes and jolted Thorf back to the present.

Now, as he looked up to see Santorini looming majestically before him, the young Serendopolis fully understood Plato's description of Atlantis; Plato's prose had the power to draw the world's curious to this spot in the Aegean Sea. "Santorini," he murmured into the wind, "that sacred island lying beneath the sun."

The Santorini vista needed no imagination to honor its magnificence. The sky was blue to the ends of the horizon, crowning the island's villas perched upon her cliffs. The bluffs of red, white, and black volcanic rock rose majestically above the deep blue of the caldera.

It appeared as if the inhabitants, not satisfied with the magnificence of this magical land, had erected churches, villas, and walls, then painted them a brilliant white, trimmed them with a blue that praised the sky above, then placed them precariously on the cliff s edge as if to dare visitors to enter.

Santorini's caldera, however, had not been an earthly architect's plan; the fourth largest volcanic eruption in Earth's history had occurred here, blowing fifty cubic miles of earth into the sky and creating a massive, basin-shaped volcanic crater. Legend has it that there once was, in the place of what is now this watery caldera, a great and wonderful metropolis that today some call Atlantis, derived from the Greek, "Island of Atlas." This so-called legend of Atlantis begged to be researched from a different point of view.

After the ship docked in the harbor, Thorf pulled out the hand-drawn map to Kafieris Apartments on the Cliff and eagerly took his place in line to debark.

It took a good deal of discipline for Thorf to concentrate on the map that would guide him to his home-to-be for the next twelve months.

He sent his suitcase and backpack up the slope on one of the donkeys for hire that awaited arriving passengers. Adjusting the shoulder strap of his laptop case, Thorf preferred to walk up the winding, cobbled path. It was breathtakingly beautiful, not to mention breathtaking—a much steeper climb than he'd imagined.

Again, the strange sensation of light-headedness engulfed him. He paused to remove his hat, hoping the burning feeling on the top of his head would go away. Then, as quickly as they had appeared, the uncomfortable feelings disappeared.

Thorf removed his windbreaker and slung it over his shoulder. For another twenty minutes, he negotiated the switchback path until he found himself at the cliff s rim where the donkey driver had placed his suitcase and backpack.

He pulled and sometimes carried his luggage up curving steps along the scenic walk. When Thorf reached a turning point on the map at Mama Thira's Restaurant, he paused to catch his breath only to have it taken away when he looked down upon the white, pink, and blue cascade of villas wedged into the cliff below.

His map directed him to take a right up more steps then onto a rubble-strewn path. The path led to a narrow, paved road that he ascended for a few minutes. Thorf felt weary from his climb, so he slowed his pace until finally ahead, higher still, he saw the sign, Kafieris Apartments on the Cliff.

Just as Dean Pringle had said, there was no one at the reception desk and the key to his room was under a pot of geraniums. It was labeled with his name and room number, 3B.

He climbed the stairs to find a tiny rooftop apartment, complete with a stunning view.

"Wow!" he said, unlocking the door. There was a terrace overlooking the caldera a few steps away, and he made a mental note to check out the view in the morning.

Thorf stepped inside his room and set everything on the little bed. He pushed aside the curtains that exposed a collage of roofs and terraces, and below that, the deep blue of the sea. Glancing at his watch, he noted there was little time to spare before his appointment with Professor Aristotle Maritimis. Now, unencumbered, he set out on foot to the village of Imerivigli.

Thorf arrived thirty-six minutes late for his appointment at Anestis Taverna. He hoped the *bouzouki* music would disguise his breathlessness. Three old men were talking and drinking at a table on the outdoor patio. One of them, upon seeing Thorf, placed both of his gnarled hands on the table and slowly stood up.

Aristotle Maritimis exclaimed, "Ah, here you are, my son," and thrust out a welcome hand to Thorf. With that jovial greeting, Thorf received the heartiest of handshakes.

"Professor Pringle told me you would look as eager as a tern who's poised for his catch of the day, and you've already got that sun-glow on your cheeks. Welcome to a bit of heaven. There may be some hell here too; avoid the hell and embrace the heaven like a true Greek! Ah, enough of my words." Aristotle motioned for Thorf to have a seat and introduced his two friends. "I'm so sorry—" Thorf made an attempt to apologize for his lateness,

Aristotle waved the rest of the apology away, then lifted a shot glass from the table. He poured its clear contents into another glass that appeared to have a small amount of water. With a convivial smile, he said, "We Greeks like to greet a friend with *ouzo*," and then he offered Thorf the drink that now held a milky emulsion. After preparing the same drink for his friends and himself, he raised his glass and smiled at Thorf. "You say 'cheers'; we say '*stin jamas.*'"

The other two men joined the toast as all three raised their glasses, pounded the table, and took a hefty swallow. Thorf followed suit, taking a more cautious amount than the others. That was a good thing. The licorice-flavored greeting burned all the way to his empty stomach, which took only a few moments to welcome the sensation.

Grizzled, sea-worn, and plagued with a painful limp that only his stubborn stoicism could mask, Aristotle Maritimis was the epitome of Santorini's "Sailor Cum Laude." His mind was full of the past and he was eager to share the adventures of his life with Thorf, and to direct him to the place where both of them could test their mastery of the curious. Aristotle invited his friends to join them as he ushered Thorf to a table inside.

The old sailor, naturally comfortable with his role as Santorini historian, ordered some wine, had Jacek, the cook, prepare his famous mussels, then began to relate his adventurous archaeological discoveries.

Late afternoon faded into evening.

"Dmitri," the professor called to the waiter. "More mussels and some eggplant. This lad needs to fatten up a bit." Aristotle refused to lose such an honored guest to an empty stomach. After the third plate of mussels and a dish of fried zucchini that Thorf wolfed down unabashedly, Aristotle paused in his narrative and patted Thorf 's shoulder. "You're like an Aegean sponge, holding more than most sponges. I mean my words, not the wine. With the *Nykteri* you are careful and take in little sips, but my words you take in big gulps. Well, maybe you are being kind to an old man, no?"

Surprised at Aristotle's keen observation, Thorf replied, "Professor Maritimis, if I remind you of a sponge, that's good. This sponge wants to be filled with the nutrients of your wisdom."

Thorf wasn't sure what part of his brain found that metaphor, but pleased with himself, he continued, "With my apology, sir, I will only sip your Santorini wine as my mind opens to the harmony of its elements."

"No apology necessary," Aristotle said.

Aware that the patrons had become unusually quiet, and he, eager to spar with this Ivy League upstart, raised his glass to toast, "It's not the spirits that open your mind, but the mind that controls the spirits to make room for the unexpected." This brought a rousing chorus of *jamas* from the crowd.

In unrehearsed unison, everyone pounded their glasses on the well-worn tables and downed the full measure of whatever they were drinking.

The evening wore on, and the crowd grew in numbers. Drink flowed freely as patrons danced the *Syrtaki* to shouts of '*Opah*' The professor became more animated, and Thorf kept his stomach full of *mezethes*, those little appetizers made with octopus, sardines, and zucchini.

As a parting measure of Grecian hospitality, Aristotle introduced Thorf to his first taste of Grecian fire water, better known as *Raki*. Thorf took one sip, smiled, and said, "*Sas efcharisto*" in his best classroom Greek.

Aristotle smiled at his student's attempt of a Grecian thank-you.

After another *Raki*, Thorf set down his empty glass. A little bleary-eyed he announced to his mentor, "I must now make room for the unexpected." He stood up and gripped Aristotle's hands in his own. "I'll need some rest for my day with you tomorrow," he said, giving his newfound friend a firm handshake. After a polite farewell nod to the locals, he went outside and found peace and quiet beneath the moonlit bougainvillea.

"Wait," Aristotle said, stumbling to catch up.

Professor Maritimis motioned for the young archaeologist to follow him into the shadow of the cascading vines. In a private corner, the old sailor whispered, "There's been a treasure discovered near the Heel Stone of Stonehenge. I've been asked to use my knowledge of Linear A to decipher a script inscribed on it. My granddaughter is bringing the artifact here tomorrow with Professor Geoffrey Devans from Bournemouth University in England. If you'd like to join us, we'll pick you up at sunrise."

"Oh, of course! Thanks!"

"I can tell already you too, like mysteries," the old seaman replied and added, "I'll see you at sunrise." He hobbled back inside.

With lively *bouzouki* music still ringing in his ears, and the thought of an unexpected adventure unfolding, Thorf staggered along the moonlit labyrinth of cobbled streets back to his rooftop apartment.

He reached the top of the stairs, fumbled for his key, and slid it into the lock. The old wooden door creaked as it moved inward, scraping along the uneven floorboards.

Odd, he thought, *I didn't turn the key … did I?*

He pushed the door open and listened—not a sound. A vision of someone with a hypodermic syringe poised to puncture him flashed through his mind. He glanced at the corner of the room where he'd left his laptop. Thankful for the full moon's light crossing the room from the window, he saw it leaning against the wall where he had left it.

"*Whew*," he said. He closed and locked the door.

Undressing was totally out of the question, and with his head reeling from stories the Raki must have embellished, Thorf fell on the bed with one last *Opah!*

They'll be here at sunrise? Is that what he told me?

Thorf closed his eyes as the soft wings of Morpheus carried him into the depths of slumber.

Part 3

In the wee hours of the morning, Thorf has been asleep for two hours since stumbling back from Anestis Taverna.

He dreamed: *The sun's too bright, I can't see clearly. What's going on outside the window? Are those protesters chanting and holding up signs? It's a crowd of strange-looking people. They're throwing things at a building! I'm so close now I can read the signs:* Stop this insane research. *What research? Why is it so bright outside, it's supposed to be night?*

Thorf tossed and turned, unable to fully awaken.

What's happening? I'm hovering close to the angry crowd. They don't see me. They're too busy burning someone … no, wait, it's an effigy. Who is it? Where is this place? Where am I?

Thorf opened his eyes and blinked. He raised himself on one elbow and saw the room basked in the light of the moon. He'd forgotten to pull the curtains closed. There was a clock near his bed. He had to squint to focus on the digits. *It's two o 'clock in the morning! The sun's still out?* He squeezed his eyes shut and swore to himself, *I've got to lay off that Raki—it's mean stuff!*

Thorf fell back on the mattress, still exhausted. His head throbbed and his eyes burned. He rolled over and covered his head with the pillow; once again he drifted into fitful sleep, the nightmares creeping back into his throbbing head.

Why isn't my body where I left it? Then he saw two men sitting in a room filled with plush furniture. Strangely attired, the men sat facing each other while talking in low voices. Their bodies were wet-looking, like they had been dipped in black ink. Their heads and necks were fitted with a blue wrap. Only their nostrils, eyes, and ears were visible through some type of transparent covering.

Thorf floated above the men and listened to their conversation.

"No, doctor," the one man said, "this isn't true. Why can't we control the ABMR-Virus? How ironic that Fellice got infected, she constantly reminded us to sanitize ourselves. I should have died, not her. I'm so empty without her! Oh, what is wrong with Authair, our world, our people?"

From his lofty point overhead, Thorf watched the person addressed as "doctor" lean over and place a comforting hand on the bereaved man's shoulder.

"Don't blame yourself, Robar. Fellice would want you to fight. Of all the theriogenologists, you understand the urgency of finding a cure. We're not sure how she contracted the virus, but she either inhaled the spores or came in contact with a carrier. Thank Olym, she suffered little."

Thorf watched as Robar lifted his head high and forced himself to sit straight. Robar stole a furtive glance left and right and whispered, "What about the rumor the Valympyons have spies among us and want to sabotage our efforts to stop the spread of the virus?"

Still hovering, Thorf watched the doctor's mouth move in response to the question, but the sound faded.

Thorf struggled to wake up. An eerie mist clouded his brain until he felt like he was falling …

The fog rolled off the ocean and dissipated quickly. The twilight seeped into view. Thorf zoomed into an unfamiliar place and time. He saw below a little girl running barefoot along the ocean's rocky shoreline holding tightly to her apron bulging with sticks.

Then, just as quickly the fog returned and Thorf heard a distant cry of "Carys, Carys, Carys!"

Thorf 's dream gave way to consciousness. *Carys, Valympyons, virus, protestors; now I'll never get to sleep.*

Thoroughly agitated and groggy, Thorf felt the room spinning, spinning so fast, he became nauseous and regretted taking that last sip of *Raki.* He struggled to stay awake, afraid the nightmares would return, but his eyes closed without his permission and he drifted back into a restless slumber.

Chapter 5
TREASURE

The year is 1600 BCE in the southern part of what is modern-day Wales.

"Carys, Carys, Carys!"

Carys didn't hear her mother's impatient calls nor feel the sting of the ocean wind that chilled her arms where the roughly woven cape no longer reached her thin wrists. Her browned and bare feet scuttled among the pebbles and sand at the water's edge. Deftly picking up pieces of dry fire-feed, she stuffed them in her apron until it would not cradle even one more fragment.

Gramps, as she was permitted to call her mother's father in private, was going to tell the story again. She, Carys, First Granddaughter, would be chosen to hold the precious, gleaming treasure made by the gods.

Having heard Gramps' story countless times, Carys could recite it word for word. But, only Honorable Grandfather had the authority to recount the tale aloud.

Clever and daring for her youthful age, the young lass found the twilight sky her loyal audience. Now, she paused in her labor, holding tightly to the folds of her bulging apron, and lifted her head to the evening sky. Her words tumbled out mimicking Gramps. Occasionally she freed a hand to dramatize her oration with a swooping gesture.

On this twilight, Carys recited her most frightful part:

The night sky over the great ocean
burst into spasms of fiery orange waves.
Not even Archdruid knew this to be his grave.

A strange moon screamed anger at dancing
red streaks that darkened and bloated its form,
grazing earth so closely that fireball became storm.

Winds swirling heat, scorched flesh and bone
tearing even the wee ones from loving arms,
as the darkness revealed Mistress Evil, her charms.

She raised from the sea a wave monstrously mean,
gazelle-like in speed reaching shore
sucking man, beast, and land's edge through her frightful door.

Twilight quickly turned to night, for Carys had taken too long to gather the fire-feed. She ran, but carefully, hoping her bare feet would not betray her tardiness with sharp stones drawing blood.

"First Granddaughter, come, you have feed enough for the full story. Sit!" With a grave look of discipline, Honorable Grandfather had spoken. He then nodded his head toward the coveted seat beside him near the fire. First Granddaughter had kept the clan waiting.

"Yes, Honorable Grandfather," Carys replied. With reddened cheeks and heaving chest, she placed her store of precious fuel on the clay hearth. Being careful not to look Honorable Grandfather in the eye, and feeling the discomfort of the other's waning patience, Carys lowered her head and seated herself on the warm straw next to Gramps.

With the readiness of a sailor waiting for the storm to subside, the young of Clan Storoch—those having seen less than 150 full moons—waited in eager anticipation for Illiachus Wynter, Honorable Grandfather, to entertain them with his story.

Stern of countenance, Illiachus began:

You are taught to call me
Guardian of the Great Water or what I prefer,
the title Honorable Grandfather Wynter.

Out of respect you do not call me,
at least when you know I am with the clan,
the most miserable name of Crippled Old Man!

Carys loved this part, for adults of Clan Storoch did not usually participate in any form of levity when addressing the children. Life was a daily struggle and Honorable Grandfather was one of a few with the gift of storytelling. He heaved up his chest and deepened his voice to emphasize the next part.

These lines on my face and this cracked old leg
were not easy to get, you know.
If you too want them, your experience must grow.

Because you are what I once was:
innocent, quiet, and never haughty,
young, curious, adventurous, but naughty.

The young listeners knew the last line by heart and said it perfectly in unison with Honorable Grandfather's voice, only each child attempted to say "naughty" the loudest.

Levity had its brief appearance and the children knew that now only the crackling of the fire must speak.

Illiachus searched through the silence of the listeners, eyeing each child thoughtfully until his gaze rested on one of the recently "naughty" children.

This time it was Carys he singled out by pointing his staff. Carys held her chin up and absorbed the laughter, knowing this was how Gramps retained his high status among the elders and respect among the children. He remained neutral, evenhanded, and fair, especially when it came to his First Granddaughter's indiscretions.

When the laughter subsided, Illiachus continued:

Many, many moons ago
when I was new to walking and wobbly would stand
mother waded in the water holding tightly to my hand.

She snatched the small fish squirming.
Their struggling no match for her keen grasp.
Vessel then full, my turn came. I did not have to ask.

It was the gift of catching fish
she wished for both her son and daughter;
nature's speed and skill with, in, and of the water.

In time my aim and grasp were sure
the fish I caught were many, from slippery eel to shad.
Then apprenticed to boat builders I sharpened blade of adz.

Willingly I chopped and hauled, splitting hard oak planks
to build our sturdy boats.
Eager my anticipation to see the vessels float.

I pumped the bellows that fired the kiln
making bronze tools that boat builders sought.
But sailing the deep waters was my burning thought.

The elders awarded a boat
old and well used, meant for someone like me
to caulk its holes, mend its mast, and sail it out to sea.

We caught many fish, the old boat and I,
carefully avoiding the storms.
Other fishing boats we together outperformed.

Manhood reached me my two hundredth moon.
A banquet ensued with a sow's slaughter.
My title bestowed: Guardian of the Great Water.

Like the seabird knows it is time
to find waters of the warming season,
so did I seek distant shores for virtuous reason.

I approached Chief Ahmet of our clan
and spoke words that caused him to laugh.
He stared looking stunned, thinking I was daft.

"Our clan is poor," is what I said.
"We see on passersby cheeks of rosy red.
The old and young of them appear to be well fed.

Our fish and oats are not enough
to keep the wee ones from growing lean.
Our young lack speed and strength; their health must be redeemed.

I will sail to the land of warm winds
where fruits in abundance grow lovely to see;
jewels picked from a bush or shaken off a tree.

There I will barter with cunning and skill,
our rock from the ground for their fruit,
bringing fresh food to our clan and a new trade route."

Chief Ahmet laughed at my youthful plan asking,
"What is this rock from the ground?
You mean this? Why it is everywhere to be found."

Illiachus got up from his seat with Carys's help and walked to the outside of the circle of listeners. Leaning over, he pretended to be looking down the edge of a cliff and held out his staff mimicking Chief Ahmet pointing to a seam of coal.

He sought the elders sage advice.
"You really think people of other clans
should buy rock that chokes? That's a hopeless plan."

They continued their argument,
each louder than the next without a gap
protesting loudly with one phrase …

At this point, the young clan members shouted the final words: *That's Pig Crap!*

Not allowing a moment to savor the children's' eager outburst. Illiachus continued:

Others with hope in my offer
overruled the skeptics as they chanted and danced
invoking Beli Mawr for my voyage to give good chance.

In a faithful boat named Windspeed
I sailed south to barter with other clans
hopeful for an offer, I tried my salesman's plan.

The people I met were friendly.
Happy to meet me they welcomed my kind,
however, my cargo they quickly declined.

These people were happily warmed
by their fire. It was for gold that they yearned.
They had no wish for noxious black rock that burned.

Could the elders be right?
Was I daft in the head with adventurous dreams?
"No," said I, "I'll ration my food and change my scheme."

It was the fifth day of the fourth moon cycle
for my boat and I at sea.
A breeze easy on the sail set my spirit free.

I gave Windspeed to set the course
and we sailed under cloudy skies to shore.
Heavy fog rolled in so dense I could see no more.

Stepping onto watery beach I shuddered
from unfamiliar dampness there.
My senses warned me of strange creatures to beware.

Then venturing forth onto dry land,
I sought tinder to spark a warming fire
and to find a safe shelter in which to retire.

I spun dry branch on ash wood thin
producing heat, then warm embers smoking.
Happy was I to have my black rocks for stoking.

Warming myself at the fire
I felt the fog begin to rise and stir the air.
A whirlwind from the north gave me to despair.

A cloud like a fire unfolding itself
with brightness all about appeared.
Out of the mist came a great wheel as the fog cleared!

The clouds lifted higher and through them
this wild creature of the sky descended,
larger far than I had ever comprehended.

It glowed the color of amber
and within the great wheel was another one.
The smaller wheel not moving while the great one spun.

Lightning flashed and the grasses on the ground
flattened in the shape of a wheel.
My warm fire was blown out. It was all so surreal!

Stretching forth from high above
a magnificent home for traveling gods.
The outer wheel whirling a greeting macabre.

It stopped within a fish's leap of Windspeed:
silently, no sound of talking,
hovering, it appeared to prepare for walking.

Four legs came forth from the inner wheel's underbelly
resting on straight feet,
golden soles like that of calf making no retreat.

The inner wheel held another
that opened revealing the color of beryl.
In stunned amazement I quickly realized my peril.

High above me through the open ring
there upon a sparkling throne was he.
a living creature sitting with his back to me.

Falling as from a dewdrop,
two other creatures emerged onto the land.
Beware, I thought, these two may have a deadly plan.

One's shoulders held a mighty butterfly chrysalis
without any wings
that whistled airy sounds like when a fairy sings.

The other appeared to have two heads and four faces,
one like a lad in front.
The other, a dragon-like creature, was the runt.

Then, strange as this was and stranger still,
the taller one removed his head.
Well, it was not a head but a cover instead.

I, being in shock, and having to look through clouds
at a sight most bizarre,
was much confused about these creatures from afar.

A fleece-like collar peeled away.
It was the runt on the shorter one's shoulder
unfurling tail with furry mane, acting bolder.

Quite a show the runt displayed
with fur of brilliant green and a curious gaze.
His big blue eyes studied me as if to appraise.

The two in silent conversation
looked from one to the other, then to me.
Their expressions were solemn, I felt I should flee.

But the short one held up a hand
gesturing for me to not run away.
Decision Maker I named him that very day.

They both approached within an arm's reach
staring curiously at me in the face.
I could not run—my legs were frozen in that place.

I felt no cold, I felt no heat,
my body appeared to have run away,
my mind the only thing that decided to stay.

My body would not leave me now!
I'd survive these creatures' attack.
They'd have to take me alive! I would not turn back.

I stared them straight into their eyes
and would not bow my head or beg for life.
Then something gentle and breezy eased my strife.

Like a feather's wispy touch
it brushed my head from one side to the other.
Next came a voice like that of a true brother.

From whom it came I did not know,
could these living creatures be Storoch kin?
Feeling stronger, I gave them my salesman's grin.

The words that I heard were familiar,
but not a mouth moved to show me who spoke.
Was this a test or a living creature's weird joke?

As I am before you this is the truth
These words of kindness to me he extends,

Distorting his voice to sound like the creature, Illiachus continued:

"Greetings, Sea Master, Izzyandteam come as friends.

Izzyandteam have observed
that Sea Master carries valuable fire glow.
Izzyandteam wish to trade Sea Master's cargo."

I rather liked these weird ones who
raised my status to Master of the Sea
so, being very clever I got them to agree.

I said, "Sea Master's fire glow
is quite precious and valuable as you know.
What do you have in trade for this precious cargo?"

A feather's touch I felt then heard,
"A sample of Sea Master's cargo to see,
with that request does Sea Master agree?"

"Izzyandteam should be quick," I
said, "Sea Master must rest for moonrise nears.
Windspeed and I sail to sea as first light appears"

I chose a large piece of my most precious and expensive
black rock that burns,
gave it to Decision Maker hoping he returns.

He reached out to take it
with a four-fingered hand, a knob in the middle.
Had he suffered a blow or was this a riddle?

His other hand I then observed
had five fingers as do I and all my clan.
Rather young, he looked a curiously bald man.

Even though a dragon runt clung around his neck
the words spoke signs of virtue.
First the feather's touch on me and then "Thank you."

True to my honor, believe me
this dragon runt's uncommonly wise,
cocked his head looking agog deep into my eyes!

I reasoned there was more to him
than casual appearance could demonstrate.
I'd pacify the dragon so not to be his bait.

They walked toward the curious dewdrop,
and bursting, it took them within.
Lifting them, the dewdrop had been made whole again.

Straight away I saw a glow from
within, as if many fireflies dancing,
then heard sounds of rejoicing and creatures prancing.

With a flash of what seemed to be
lightning, beside me two creatures appeared.
Decision Maker held out his hand as I cheered!

He offered me a glittering object;
a huge spool of finely spun gold.
My thoughts quickly framed a clever plan to unfold.

I saw the creatures weren't trained
in earthly ways of how to fill their coffer,
so I politely declined their meager offer.

"Thank you, but Sea Master's fire glow
is much too precious for such a little gold."
Surprised they were but wished for me to be consoled.

They hurriedly rose to their mystical home
leaving me with gold so fine.
My belly being empty, I prepared to dine.

I settled down sipping clear water
and eating fish from my provisions.
Suddenly frightful cries challenged my decisions.

A high-pitched voice of a lass in distress
sent me jumping to my feet,
dropping the tasty fish for scavengers to eat.

Sounds unlike man, animal, wind, or water
filled the silence of the sea.
Quick decision I must make: should I stay or flee!

My answer came when I looked down
upon the gleaming treasure in my hand.
I'd stay and face my fate. Their wrath I would withstand!

Soon the noises were no more,
welcomed silence to the land again returned.
As the full moon rose, a plan within me churned.

The creatures appeared on the ground
and approached to bargain in their form,
handing to me three lumps of sparkling gold, still warm.

I felt a wispy touch of feather
and words most welcome to my ear,
"Will Sea Master take this gold offer as sincere?"

This was part one of the bargain
I could barely keep from celebrating.
Part two was nine more loads with each trip rotating.

They required the black rock delivered,
so mysterious work could be done
on the island of caves that lies toward the setting sun.

This bargain was one to snatch up
before the naïve creatures changed their minds.
I proposed a clever contract as one that binds.

I said, "Yes, if upon each of my deliveries
at such a place remote
you'll supply labor to remove it from my boat."

Surely, they would not expect
Master of the Sea to toil beneath his rank.
Izzyandteam agreed before my offer sank.

For each delivery I would receive
four spools of sparkling gold as pay;
additionally, the cargo they would haul away.

I sensed these creatures were ripe for the picking
so not wanting to mislead,
to this honorable contract I quickly agreed!

My word of honor was then given
to keep the creatures unidentified
and the delivery location I'd have to hide.

A magic box to guide my way
was a welcome gift they offered to me
if I promised to keep this box in secrecy.

The box had parts that moved and turned
skillfully crafted but unknown to me.
Engraved symbols showed how to make a safe journey.

The magic box would point my way
and show me where to sail the precious load.
Excitedly I quickly learned its secret code.

The parts moved as I asked it
to show the right direction for my sail.
It followed the sun, moon, or stars, and would not fail.

This ingenious tool in my hand
would be challenging to keep undisclosed.
Quite clever would be the story I must compose.

I could invent a storytalk
that my clansmen would readily believe,
unlike the truth, no imagination could conceive.

The story I'd tell would be
of distant clans that wanted my precious load.
Their caves were cold. They welcomed my black rocks that glowed.

"Where did their gold come from?" my
clansmen would ask, thinking my story not true.
I'd say, "Their caves had much gold, but their lips were blue."

Having conducted their business,
the living creatures returned to the wheel.
The dewdrop lifted them, ending the ordeal.

In awe I watched this magnificent ship of the sky
hide its sturdy feet,
and ascend with a quietly speedy retreat.

It vanished through the thickening clouds.
Was this a specter that the gods had sent?
I marveled at the fortune of such a chance event.

At first light, I took my leave commanding,
"Find Island of Caves."
The magic box guided me safely through the waves.

Nearing the strange lush green island,
I saw the creatures waving from the shore.
Their ingenious tool did the lifting I abhor.

It was a mountain of sharp-edged stones
they'd built with odd standing logs and puffing smoke.
They offered me a warm rest with no fire to stoke.

I bid them farewell and headed
toward the rising sun for jewels from the tree.
With fresh fruit and gold to spare, my clan welcomed me.

The chief and elders gathered round
pleading to hear of my fruitful mission.
To this request, I humbly gave my rendition.

I told of how Windspeed and I
survived huge crashing waves and burning sun,
and how I met strange bald creatures with a dragon.

The tale I wove was wondrously captivating
and all thought it true.
Of the actual story …

Illiachus paused allowing the chorus of eager participants to complete the line:

"… they didn't have a clue!"

Fifty moons passed as I made
many trips returning with fresh fruit and gold.
Chief Ahmet honored me for the cargo I'd sold.

The Clan Storoch Award for the
Utilization of Black Rock that Burns
was my tribute for many successful returns.

The dearest prize was given to me by my wife Rhea
as these words she spoke,
"My love for you is woven into this warm cloak."

She took from my shoulders the tattered wrap
that had served me well through the years.
Feeling the warmth of her weave, I was brought to tears.

Not only I, but all of our
clan marveled at Rhea's fitting design.
Tiny fishes swimming woven nettle so fine.

When I'd been off sailing she'd dyed the nettle red
then wove with faithful dispatch.
She did this with cunning I myself couldn't match.

Look closely at this living warmth
I wear as comfort to my weary bones.
Rhea's talent and brilliance it clearly condones.

Illiachus lifted the cloak and caressed it to his cheek, then carefully removed the precious garment and handed it to Carys who held it lovingly and walked around the circle of eager children, allowing them to closely inspect the craftsmanship of an honored ancestor.

He continued:

This would be my last chance
Rhea's smile to see and precious times with her to share.
The gods would snatch her up leaving me to despair.

At first light we walked together to the water's edge.
She bid me safe return.
Lighthearted we, this final trip gave us no concern.

I arrived as usual to the island
where smoking monuments they'd made.
This time no smoke in the sky; I was afraid!

So still it was, and no magic lift
to remove my cargo from Windspeed.
I anchored my boat wondering if I should leave.

A foreboding told me that something
amiss had befallen my loyal friends.
If they needed rescue, my help I would extend.

Walking onto land I came upon an engraved picture stone,
meant to be found.
It was leaning against a big rock on the ground.

Upon close examination
I found that it was created for me
with a likeness of Windspeed drawn masterfully.

No time to be pleased at all
because there among the images was me.
Not Illiachus as Illiachus wants to be!

A drawing of my body with
blood all about warned me of what to do,
to anchor Windspeed where the wind would not pursue.

With my back to the setting sun
I was to climb and enter a rock cave.
Would this lonely forbidden place become my grave?

Ahh, but just as I was to throw away
the clever story of my doom,
a vision of glittering gold took away the gloom.

Pictured with masterful art,
there on a cave floor were the sparkling gold spools,
my final payment more precious than jewels.

I would follow instructions of the vivid pictures
engraved in hard clay.
I hoped to survive to enjoy another day.

The sketches showed a map
that directed me into a hidden rock cave.
There I found the gold, but must climb to be saved.

Leaving the gold behind, I climbed far up
following a hazy light beam
over a jagged rocky path as in a bad dream.

The light slowly grew brighter
the farther I wound up and through the damp cave.
It was eerie and frightening. I had to be brave.

The path was no more. I had come to the end
where light from above gave hope,
for on a smooth stone were rations to help me cope.

On the floor at my feet was a vessel
with cool water for me to drink,
and strange spongy fishes of red, yellow, and pink.

A mystery these fish to eat
with a sweetness like that of ripened fruit.
That they eased my hunger was no dispute.

I chewed and swallowed every one
then sat against the wall and closed my eyes.
Sleep came quickly bringing dreams of menacing skies.

I awoke to a world of darkness
feeling the cold of the rock where I sat.
So quiet it was, not even the sound of a bat.

Suddenly a brightness appeared
through the opening above me
bringing the creatures' prophesized catastrophe.

The night sky over the great ocean
burst into spasms of fiery orange waves.
Not even Archdruid knew this to be his grave.

A strange moon screamed anger at dancing red streaks
that darkened and bloated its form
grazing earth so closely that fireball became storm.

Winds swirling heat, scorched flesh and bone
tearing even the wee ones from loving arms
as the darkness revealed Mistress Evil, her charms.

She raised from the sea a wave
monstrously mean, gazelle-like in speed reaching shore,
sucking man, beast and land's edge through her frightful door.

Carys thrilled to hear Gramps recite this part of the story and at the same time worried about her grandfather who tried not to show he was in pain. Many sundowns, fewer now, he would struggle to get up from his warm place at the fire, and with Carys' help, hobble away from the fire's light; one arm curling around First Granddaughter's shoulder, and the other pointing to the first star on the horizon.

Gramps taught Carys his knowledge of the night sky. On days when feeling stronger he would show Carys how to find the best fire feed and she would beg him to tell her again about the precious treasure, and sometimes, just a few times, Gramps would tell Carys to hurry to the secret hiding place and bring The Treasure to him. Then, with it snuggled safely in her arms, Gramps would begin his storytalk.

But, tonight's storytalk included all the clan's children. Carys waited patiently, knowing she would soon hold The Treasure once more.

Honorable Grandfather continued:

I will never forget Thor's ravenous anger
that ripped our world apart.
For at this moment the sound still tears at my heart.

Then, I woke to a silence of cavernous depth
that seemed an eerie void.
Was it my two ears, had they also been destroyed?

I snapped my fingers together
one time sharply as each ear took its turn.
It worked so well the slightest snap I could discern.

How long had I lain upon the cave's hard floor?
There was no way of knowing.
Something vile had crushed my leg and left blood flowing.

Had the terrible shaking dislodged a rock
and tumbled it out from the wall
heavy enough to splinter muscle, bone, and all?

My leg felt a fire within and
like an unruly young lad of our clan
it refused to obey my repeated command.

"Move," I demanded out loud in the dark,
but the fire burned deep through the skin.
Illiachus will triumph and pain shall not win!

I groped in the dark to find the path
that had led me to this lofty height.
Suddenly I saw a faint bluish blinking light.

Was this a friendly fairy's beam
designed to guide me safely from this room,
or could it be an evil specter of my doom?

One then two, then many, many shimmering dots of brightness
lit my way.
No longer did I fear my path would go astray.

These glowing spirits spread above
a pleasing wonder to my weary eyes,
comforting me like a blanket of starlit skies.

With two arms and one good leg,
I crawled along the damp and rocky floor.
The bleeding ceased. I felt the burning pain no more.

Sharp edges of small rocks cut through my hands
and the flesh of my one good knee.
The path wound left then right, difficult to foresee.

How long? I asked myself as down the steeply sloping path
I slowly crawled.
It had been night before the storm, as I'd recalled.

Each turn I took yet difficult
showed fewer twinkles on the walls about.
A beam of yellow grew, pointing me the way out.

Two tired arms and one bruised knee
dragged me through the rocky descent to full light.
The brightness lifted my spirit to a new height

Down around and farther did I pull my leg
with tired forearms dripping blood.
Then to find the door's path full of sticky mud.

Amidst the slime I found the gold,
being so heavy I thought to leave it there.
But to our clan such thoughtlessness would be unfair.

I tied the drawstring round my belt
and looked upon the outside world of light.
Fallen limbs at the entrance added to my plight.

But no! A branch, one to hold my body's weight
was there for me to take!
I would choose a strong one and use my flint to shape.

A sturdy stick of a good length
I quickly found to help me stand upright.
I could not find my flint pouch, it was out of sight.

The pouch must have torn off
as I dragged it over sharp rocks on the bumpy way.
The crude stick, as it was, must do for the day.

It held me straight and I felt delight
to breathe the fresh air, but what was there?
Fallen trees, piles of rocks, and branches everywhere.

Frighteningly quiet no song of bird,
no chattering of woodland creature.
The lovely scene before, now a ravaged feature.

Was it a mirage or a gift from the gods
that Windspeed was in plain sight?
There in calm water she stood perfectly upright.

The sight of my boat gave me hope
that I'd be able to sail safely home.
I was thankful to be alive and feel the sea's foam.

Grateful to see the bright blue sky,
I knew the Living Creatures saved my life.
How could I thank them? Did they too survive the strife?

Rhea, mother of my first-born
Caryn, our wee one, what has happened to them?
I must return to help all survive this mayhem.

There was little time to wonder more,
for the sun was low and fading fast.
I hobbled as I could to reach Windspeed at last.

I had to get to the coil of hemp
to bind a stick securely to my leg.
It lay on Windspeed's deck next to the water keg.

I tossed the bag over the side of the boat,
freeing me of the gold's weight.
First, the crutch hit the deck, then Windspeed's first mate.

I will admit, landing on the wood planks
was a most unwelcome feat.
The pain returned a torment I would not repeat.

The coiled hemp I grabbed then righted myself,
but how could I cut it to size?
I scanned the boat for something I could improvise.

Not a thing there would satisfy.
Perhaps some flint had washed up on the shore.
Climbing out of Windspeed was movement I'd deplore.

Even with a careful lift of my injured leg,
the pain was something cruel.
That, I would endure for the proper cutting tool.

Looking around amongst the debris,
I chanced to see a sparkling object.
I limped a bit closer, the item to inspect.

Such a brilliance coming from its hiding place
amongst many shells and fallen trees.
I pried it with my stick and it came out with ease.

A golden rim it had with shape of half a moon
and edge sharper than flint.
Had the living creatures lost it as they went?

No mere mortal could have fashioned
this object from the earth or from the sea.
What marvelous tool was this intended to be?

This was her signal; tonight Carys was the one to display The Treasure as had other children in her moon's phase been awarded this distinction. She rose from her seat next to Gramps and helped him to stand. Carys then knelt and brushed aside the straw on which Gramps had been sitting, exposing a leather sheath that held The Treasure. She carefully removed The Treasure from its protective cover and replaced the straw. With the cherished object held firmly to her chest, Carys gingerly sat down again.

Secured by his staff, Illiachus continued:

Closely examining it I saw symbols in black
between gold and red curves.
A fanciful tale of events I did observe.

Near the jagged edge in the center
were two figures much larger in size.
It being incomplete, the meaning was disguised.

Illiachus gestured in the air the letters *I* and *Z*, and Carys held the plate high, turning it in all directions for everyone to see. Illiachus continued:

Could it have been the terrible chaos
that created the jagged side?
Something hard struck the object, making it divide.

Sparkling specks on front and back
dancing all about was the effect it gave.
Its jagged edge looked sharp enough the rope to shave.

The hemp was tough and thick
made to firmly hold a sail in winds that thrash.
Surprisingly it cleaved the rope with one quick slash!

Illiachus slashed his arm in the air as the young lads and lasses acted out their own energetic versions of severing the tough strands.

The hemp now of proper length,
I quickly separated its twisted strands.
Binding my leg was hard to do with bloody hands.

Boarding Windspeed caused me less pain
with my securely bound but injured leg
I carefully tied the tool to the water keg.

Eager was I to sail out to sea,
but where was my magic box?
It must have toppled out from wave's turbulent shocks.

Why should I need the magic box,
being the Master of the Sea?
I, Illiachus, would sail home without difficulty.

Happily a favorable wind
filled Windspeed's sail and sent me on our way.
The Island of Caves never more would I survey.

My faithful boat and I sailed straight home
not once having to change our course,
hoping my clan had survived the wind's deadly force.

Upon my arrival
I found the ocean that once had kept our clan alive,
in one cataclysmic event, their lives deprived.

Honorable Grandfather turned to Carys and nodded his head. It was her signal to stand.

She stood tall and mirrored her grandfather's solemn expression.

"First Granddaughter," he said, after placing his gnarled hand on her head, "this is your final storytalk as a child. You have earned the privilege of keeping The Treasure safe. You have reached the age of 150 moons and have grown to learn the world of women."

He paused and turned to look at the young audience, making sure all were attentive, then turned back to Carys. "As First Granddaughter of Illiachus Wynter, you are now awarded the honor of carrying on the storytalk tradition of The Treasure, upon my entering into the After World.

I hereby assign you to be the Keeper of the Treasure, to learn the story by heart, to repeat it only while in my presence, and to swear you will never change a word that you have heard me talk."

He removed his hand from Carys's head and steadied himself with both hands on his staff then looked gravely at his first granddaughter as he spoke, "Do you so swear by Arianrhod, First Granddaughter?"

Carys was not prepared for this request. She was overwhelmed by the magnitude of the responsibility. She had been taught about the sky goddess, Arianrhod, keeper of the circling silver wheel of stars.

She stood with shaking knees holding The Treasure fast to her chest, Carys's heart was pounding as the words tumbled from her soul, "Honorable Grandfather Wynter, Guardian of the Great Water, you have prepared me to do many things in this difficult but wondrous life. There is much yet for me to learn from you. I will be your willing student, your protégé, and your devoted First Granddaughter. I swear by Arianrhod to keep The Treasure safe, to learn the story by heart, to repeat it while only in your presence, and to never change a word that you have talked."

Her oath completed, Carys held The Treasure high, raising it for all to see. A spiritual moment flooded her soul; the serenity reflected in her eyes. She bowed her head, and using her free hand grasped the thick, curly hair at the nape of her neck. The other hand thrust the razor's sharp edge of The Treasure through the mass of tresses, severing every strand.

The children gasped!

Understanding the profound act of humility his granddaughter had performed, Illiachus reached for Carys's hand, opened her fingers, and reverently gathered the mass of red curls in into his palm. He looked into her eyes with moisture in his own and said, "First Granddaughter, your oath and your sacrifice are honey to the gods. We shall celebrate at full moon your humble transformation."

While the children cheered the celebration that was to bring dancing, good food, and a day of happiness, Carys again parted the straw and placed The Treasure securely inside its protective home. When the sounds of merriment died down, the children sat silent once again, eagerly awaiting the final moments of the story. The festive moment lifted Illiachus's spirit, and with renewed vigor he stood straight and tall for the culmination of the tale.

As Windspeed sailed swiftly to shore,
young lads in ragged clothing greeted me.
So desperately hoping for fruit from the tree.

They jumped aboard the boat and hoisted me on their shoulders,
seeing I could not run.
Obvious to me that their lives had been undone.

A makeshift shelter the young lads had made
to keep the survivors alive.
No elders were left whose wisdom they could derive.

I spoke no words but scanned the faces of our clan
huddled near the fire.
An infant cried. She awakened my one desire.

To know of Rhea was all I cared
at this moment of stark reality.
I hesitated to ask the question, "Where is she?"

A young lass stepped forward with babe in her arms.
She handed the wee one to me.
"Your daughter Caryn saved by Rhea who died in the sea."

My daughter, my Caryn, no mother
to show her the woman's role of our clan.
For this wee one I would have a nurturing plan.

In that moment I felt weak in the head,
a feeling for me to keep below.
Illiachus must not allow sorrow to show.

I, the elder now left to guide
and comfort the people of our clan
felt humbled in the presence of each young man.

So many of our good people
had been sucked into the raging storm.
Selfless acts of heroism brave lads had performed.

They taught me that the salesman's grin
is superficial in the face of grief,
to move beyond my pain for another's relief.

That if you lose the one you love,
you have but your very own life to live.
Take that life and make of it a living gift to give.

The listeners sat silent, intently watching Honorable Grandfather. Illiachus hobbled away, feigning the end of his storytalk, then stopped and turned back to the eager children, his eyes twinkled as he spoke:

But wait! Listen closely. There's an
important message for you I must decree.
Be clever and courageous, but never naughty.

Live every day worthwhile
by choosing noble goals that will compel,
and then become the story you someday will tell.

Carys rushed to Gramps' side. He reached out and put his arm around her. She felt the warmth of the tattered cloak on her shoulders and the majesty of his presence. As they silently walked side by side under the stars, she thought about the power of the lines, "The night sky over the great ocean burst into spasms of fiery orange waves. Not even Archdruid knew this to be his …" a tightening of Gramps' arm on her shoulder suddenly brought Carys out of her inattention. Gramps was tired and she moved closer to support his frail body, but she had no way of knowing she would become the sole keeper of The Treasure before the next full moon.

HOUSE RULES

If you open it, close it.
If you turn it on, turn it off.
If you unlock it, lock it.
If you break it, repair it.
If you borrow it, return it.
If you use it, don't abuse it.
If you make a mess, clean it up.
If you move it, put it back.
If you don't know how to operate it, leave it alone.
If you don't know something, ask someone who does.

PH

Dyzzleberry Dictionary
Iz~ The Izzy Story: Book 1, Encounters

A Great Wheel: Graviton 1, the spaceship seen by Illiachus in Ch. 5.

ABMR-Virus: A plus B Merged Retro-Virus—A deadly virus found on the Olympyon hemisphere of Planet Authair. See Ch. 4.

Algorithm: A process or set of rules to be followed in calculations. In Iz~ Cimi Nuja is referred to as the "Princess of Algorithms."

Allele: One of many genes attached to chromosomes that are responsible for determining an individual's characteristics. Thorf Serendopolis has a strange allele on his DNA. See Ch. 4.

AMS Radiocarbon Dating: Accelerator mass spectrometry method for determining the amount of Carbon Fourteen isotope in a sample which will establish the sample's age. See Ch. 3.

An Olym: A unit of time on Planet Authair equivalent to 100 minutes Earth time. Ten minutes of Earth time is equal to 0.1 olym.

Angry Botts of Authair: A game the botts and desbotts play in IZ~. Botts, Botty and Clyde, become addicted to playing the game and that gets them into trouble on their trip to MBG21 in spaceship Graviton 1.

Aquaglow: A noun used by Authairians to express a vision and or feeling of peace and beauty—example, "The evening left an aquaglow of memories."

Archdruid: The top official of the fictional ancient Welsh Storoch clan. See Ch. 5.

Arianrhod: The Moon-mother goddess of Celtic Mythology known as the keeper of the silver wheel that descends into the sea. See Ch. 5.

Atlantis: The prehistoric mythical home of an advanced culture alleged to have lived in the area of the Mediterranean Sea. Thorf discusses Atlantis in Ch. 4.

Aurora Tornadoes: Electromagnetic fields at the poles on Planet Authair. They funnel in cosmic radiation from Authair's suns Olym and Valym, creating a spiraling rainbow of colors beautiful to see, but deadly to approach. They generate a unique energy field that Authairians use in communication.

Authairian: An advanced species of intelligent beings that evolved on Planet Authair. The Authairians, both male and female resemble Earthlings with some exceptions. They have small ears and no hair on the body. Some have eyebrows and lashes. Cimi Nuja is an exception to the baldness trait. She has a tuft of hair at the top of her head. The male Authairians have four fingers on one hand. Where the middle finger would be there is a joint. This male feature develops into a hinge attached to a weapon or claw as the male matures. Authairians are hatched, not born. They socialize much in the same way as present-day Earthlings. You can see images of Authairians on our website at http://www.theizzystory.com/characters/

Biological Hazard Symbol: This symbol with "BSL 5" label identifies any area, room, office, or building to have as the highest level of safety precaution. BSL 5 was assigned to Ursula von Mengleborts's virology laboratory on spaceship Ragnarock.

Black Rock That Burns: This is coal. Illiachus Wynter attempts to sell his Black Rock That Burns. See Ch. 5.

Botty and Clyde: Two robots that travel to MBG21 aboard Graviton 1. Their addiction to playing the game *Angry Botts of Authair* gets them into trouble.

Bournemouth University: A university located in Dorset, England. It's the university Dee attends in Ch. 3.

Brainprint: A unique electromagnetic field generated by each individual's brain. The Authairian's brainprint is programmed into that individual's DB for security.

Brown Dwarf: A substellar object that roams freely in outer space. It is too low in mass to sustain hydrogen fusion like our sun. See Ch. 5.

Claw: This is a biological weapon of the male Authairian. The claw develops from DNA triggers in the male as he matures. It is usually found on the right hand where the middle finger would normally be. In that place there is a callused knob-like hinge used to activate the embedded knife-like claw. A tough enclosure of skin similar to a zipper opens the length of the forearm to expose the claw. When the mature male activates the claw, it whips out similar to the action of a switchblade and locks in place at the joint. The four fingers then close around the base of the claw to provide accuracy of aim and force. At this point, the claw resembles a sword and becomes a deadly weapon. This will be in a future edition of IZ~.

Collared Urn: A style of pottery characteristic of the Bronze Age in present-day England. These urns have a large collar-like opening on top, and they are devoid of handles. Tasy finds a collared urn. See Ch. 3.

Cosmic String: Kurl Tszargon with the help of Cimi Nuja manages to create a way for the ABMR-Virus team to depart Planet Authair, spend five Earth years away while only having been gone one day of Authair time. They displaced time by circling around cosmic strings.

Costa Coffee: A popular brand of coffee in England. It is the slogan on the Costa cup that gives Dee an aha moment! See Ch. 3.

CRT-A1-Triage: Code on the Dyzzleberry Communicator. Cimi uses it in Ch. 1.

Ddwlem: Ddwlem is the pseudonym of the authors of Iz~ The Izzy Story. It is a combination of the initials for D. Duayne Whitehurst and Lucille E. Mayton. It's pronounced *dwel' em* and rhymes with bellum as in antebellum.

Desbott: Desbotts are machines created to care for and secure the army of Notouchims that Ursula von Menglebort has genetically created to kill off the Olympyons. The desbott's job is to secure the Notouchims in their confined area, deliver life support supplies to them, sanitize the cells and to maintain the visual surveillance hologram system aboard Ragnarock.

Double Trouble Bubble Gum: The bubble gum that Cimi Nuja chews to calm down and focus. She claims that it gives her a creative edge. For every one of her creative moments she pops a bubble. The gum is naturally black because it contains multiwalled carbon nano tubes that also give it extra strength.

Dyzzleberry Communicator: Authairians have a device called the Dyzzleberry Communicator or DB. Its name came from the Dyzzleberry plant that develops a vivid red berry and grows near the poles on Planet Authair. The DB has an indicator light that glows red when in active communication mode. Its owner texts or speaks a message and the DB relays that message over any distance to the intended recipient's brain. The recipient receives this mental message through the unique field created by the aurora tornadoes. It was discovered that energy created by this field could be harnessed through the DB technology and used for planetary communication. The DB is programmed to activate the glial cells of the recipient's brain.

Every DB owner must have his or her brainprint programmed into the device for the glial cells to pick up the transmission. Glialpathing is the term for communicating this way. The DB has an embedded unit that can be retracted or exposed when activated. It then becomes a powerful telescopic camera as well as a projector. The DB has evolved to a micro-thin, flexible, organic-like device that is attached (with a gel-like glue) to a convenient spot on the body. Once adhered to the body, the device instantly reads the DNA profile and compares it to the one that has been programmed in it. The DB will only operate for authorized wearers.

Dyzzleberry Dictionary: The cloud source of all knowledge on Planet Authair. It is accessed by the Dyzzleberry Communicator, as well as other media.

E Two Two: Robotic emergency message indicating an intruder at the PHI. See Ch. 1.

Early Bronze Age: The period in Earth's history in which bronze was first used in tool manufacture. In Wales it is estimated to be from 2500 to 1400 BCE. See Ch. 3.

Earthlings: Inhabitants of Earth as referred to by the Authairians who visited there.

Equapyon Range: The mountain range that encircles Planet Authair at its equator defining the geographic border between the Olympyon and Valympyon civilizations.

Glialpath: Direct communication to Authairian brain cells through a DB using the unique energy field created by the aurora tornadoes on Planet Authair. See Ch. 1.

Gnarlythorn: A dense tree-like shrub that covers large areas on Planet Authair. It is dangerous because of its sharp thorns that protrude from every imaginable angle. However, its blossoms produce nectar that is among the most sought-after plant substance on the planet. Leachim finds himself in a grim situation while trying to negotiate the gnarlythorns at Gore Andriol's deadly orders. You will find this episode in a future edition.

Graviton 1: An advanced spaceship developed by the Olympyons on Planet Authair. It is capable of traveling through the dark energy field faster than the speed of light.

Growing Lab: There are two different growing labs. One is the area in Graviton 1 that provides for the growing of food for the crew. The other area is a vast land on the property of the Ponce Heidon Institute of Genetics for the development of plant species. Both growing labs are run by Chico Quwattle.

Hearts: Authairians have two hearts; one to pump the blood to the lungs to receive oxygen and the other to pump the oxygenated blood around the body.

Hidden Gems: Nuggets of information that add background information to story elements or to characters. Find them at: http://www.theizzystory.com/hidden-gems/

House Rules: Ponce Heidon established Rules of Organization for his employees of The Ponce Heidon Institute of Genetics. He called these the House Rules. See "House Rules."

Impervious Body Skin: Protective body covering, including a facial bubble that protects the wearer from viral infection. Such a skin is what Robar is wearing in Thorf 's dream. See Ch. 4.

Island of Caves: Sao Miquel Island, the largest of the volcanic islands in the Azores. The island is known for its proliferation of caves and lava tubes. Illiachus experiences a catastrophe while he is on the Island of Caves. See Ch. 5.

Kan-Du: A form of martial arts popular on Planet Authair. Kan-Du is only performed by Authairian males who are trained to use their claw as a defensive weapon in life-death situations. Kurl Tszargon developed the technique and taught Gore Andriol who then joined Mumba Zola's army.

Laverstock: A small village located in Wiltshire, England, twelve miles from Stonehenge. Dee lives in an apartment in Laverstock. See Ch. 3.

Linear A Script: An undeciphered ancient hieroglyphic script used in Minoan writings. Aristotle Maritimis is asked to decipher an unknown script found on an artifact from Stonehenge. See Ch. 4.

Linear B Script: A deciphered syllabic script used for writing in Mycenaean Greece about 1400 BCE. See Ch. 3.

Magic Box: Strikingly similar to the Antikythera Mechanism found near the island of Antikythera in the Mediterranean Sea. Illiachus is given a magical box to guide him to the Island of Caves. See Ch. 5.

Magnelev: A device developed by Authairians to counter the force of gravity.

Magnetic Levitation: A phenomenon that describes how Authairians counter the force of gravity using Planet Authair's strong magnetic fields.

MBG21: The code used by the Olympyons to identify Earth. Only Cimi Nuja knows the true meaning of each letter, as revealed in a sequel to this book.

Morphload: An Authairian verb meaning to display from a communication device such as a Dyzzleberry Communicator, a live-action holographic image. For example, Cimi might say this while demonstrating her newly designed DB: "Wow, an Olymfab morphload from my DB. Look at that Chico, Izzy's licking up the last crumb of his tuna broccoli treat!"

Multiwalled carbon nanotubes: Multiple walled layers (concentric tubes) of single sheets of graphite (graphene). Cimi suspects her bubble gum has some special qualities. See Ch. 3.

National Public Telepathy: NPT is the public service communication network of Planet Authair. They have no need for radio or television transmissions as NPT transmits through a unique energy field generated between the Aurora tornadoes at the two poles of the planet. Network information is received by Dyzzleberry Communicators (DBs) that all Authairians possess. The DB retransmits the information directly to the glial cells of Authairian's brains as telepathic messages. Therefore public information is available at all times and at all locations whenever an Authairian desires to tune in.

Neurons: Electrically excitable cells that process and transmit information through electrical and chemical signals. See Ch.1.

Notouchims: Notouchims are living creatures created in the laboratory by Ursula von Menglebort. She created them as weapons to kill enemies of Valympyons and to conquer the Olympyons. A lethal substance comes out of their pores and is fatal to the touch. Dr. von Menglebort manipulated genes so that the fear receptors in the brains of Notouchims are turned off. In physical appearance they resemble humans who have curly blond hair, stocky arms and legs and are stunted in growth.

Olym: Planet Authair's southern sun. The people on Planet Authair who live under Olym's rays are called Olympyons. Olym is also revered as a god to some Authairians. See Ch.4.

Olymfab: An expression in Authairian Speak that means fabulously of Olympic standards. It's synonym in Earth Speak is "awesome." Cimi Nuja likes to use the expression. "That's Olymfab!" See Ch. 2.

Olympya: Southern hemisphere of planet Authair and home of The Good in IZ~.

Olympyon: A citizen of Olympya. Ponce, Dorf, Cimi, Kurl, Robar, Phed, and Izzy are Olympyons. Chico was originally a Valympyon but fled to Olympya.

PAUSN: Translates to Planet Authair Universal Serial Number. It is similar to the US Library of Congress identification code ISBN.

PCR Lab: There is a PCR lab aboard both spaceships, Graviton 1 and Ragnarock. PCR, polymerase chain reaction, is a scientific technique in molecular biology to amplify a single or a few copies of a piece of DNA by several orders of magnitude, which generates thousands to millions of copies of a particular DNA sequence. Dorf Tzeus performs his humanitarian work in Graviton 1's PCR lab and Ursula von Menglebort performs her evil work in Ragnarock's PCR lab.

PHI: Ponce Heidon Institute for genetic research. It is on Planet Authair in the city of Olymopos. This is where The Good begin developing a cure for the ABMR-Virus.

PHI:104: Sample code on the Dyzzleberry Communicator used to establish communication with an employee of the PHI.

Pixelated: A description that Kurl Tszargon gives to Cimi Nuja because of her obsession with breaking information into units such as pixels.

Planet Authair: Planet Authair is pronounced *out there.* It is the home of our characters who are classified as The Good and The Bad. It is located on the outer rim of our Milky Way Galaxy and revolves in an orbit between two stars of a binary star system. On Planet Authair, there are no nights. The Equapyon Mountain Range circles the entire planet at its equator.

Planet Authair—Orbit: Authair's orbit revolves around the center of gravity of two stars in a triple star system. The two primary stars controlling Authair' s orbit, each on opposite hemispheres of Planet Authair, are Olym and Valym. Proxi is the third and much more distant star that is equally distant to both Olym and Valym. The effect of Proxi on Authair's orbit is slight but important for Authair's stability. Authair's orbit resembles an invisible Ferris wheel. Directly perpendicular to the hub of this invisible Ferris wheel, far into space, we see Olym on one side and Valym on the other side of the imaginary hub. Much farther out in space, directly in line with the imaginary turning rim of the Ferris wheel, is the star Proxi.

Planet Midden: A myth about a celestial body called Planet Midden has been recounted through the ages by Authairians. It explains how their ancestors developed a method to dispose of their refuse. They would send it on the backs of giant flying dragons to a celestial body orbiting their planet. They called this celestial body Planet Midden. As each dragon arrived on Planet Midden, it would find a fresh open area for depositing the load, then fly to an old deposit that had ripened and turned into a wonderful feast for a tired and hungry dragon. After feasting and a sleep cycle of rest, the dragon would return to Planet Authair to continue the recycling process. Planet Midden today is said to be lush and lovely with shimmering-winged miniature dragons thriving on the nectar of flowering succulents.

Plasma Furnace: A furnace that uses ionized hydrogen and plasma to heat objects tens of thousands of degrees. See Ch. 2.

Plexi: An extremely strong polymeric construction material. See Ch. 1.

Ponce Heidon Institute: An institute (PHI) for genetic research established by Ponce Heidon through the request and support of the Olympyon government to create a cure for the ABMR-Virus. See Ch. 1.

Portal: The celestial window created by the Thorium Lensing Device, TLD, that allows entry and exit into the dark energy field in space.

Proxi: Of the three suns affecting Planet Authair's orbit, Proxi is the one farthest away, creating the apex in space of an imaginary triangle with Olym and Valym.

Quindar Tone: A sound that indicates voice transmission is about to begin between a spacecraft and its tower operators.

Ragnarock: This is the Valympyon's space ship. They designed and built it from stolen plans of Graviton 1.

Ralkids: Tall, wispy trees with shimmering spider-web shaped leaves, found primarily on the Valympyon hemisphere of Planet Authair.

RCDG1M: This stands for Ragnarock Chase and Destroy Graviton 1 Mission. It's the mission commanded by Mumba Zola.

RFI: Rosaland Franklin Institute of Genetics is a fictional laboratory where Thorf Serendopolis had his blood type identified as ABX. See Ch. 4.

Safety Shell: The device attached to the seats on Graviton 1 that secures the occupant into a safe position during liftoff, landing, through portals of the dark energy field and during other potentially hazardous travel conditions.

SAVED: The code for Successful Antivirus Effectively Developed that Dorf Tzeus and Robar Gimmel use in a future edition of IZ~ as the signal for distribution preparation of the ABMR-Virus vaccine.

Security Lounge: This is the seating in Graviton 1's command center that each crewmember occupies while at work. The crewmembers are secured to their seats when extra precaution is necessary during flight. It contains the safety shell that is stored inside the base of the seat during normal flight conditions.

Sleep Cycle: That period of time designated by Authairians for rest since Planet Authair has perpetual daylight. Authairians have eyelids that block out specific levels of illumination. When they close their eyes completely, a gel-like substance seals the upper eyelid to the lower lid.

Squreep: Onomatopoeia for the Quindar tone.

Stunfire: A small weapon that immobilizes the victim without deadly force. It is used for protection by the Olympyons on Planet Authair. See Ch. 1.

The Bad: The following characters in Iz~ The Izzy Story: Ursula von Menglebort, Gore Andriol, Leachim Ztulk, Mumba

Zola, and Jeeves who is kindhearted and well trained but must obey the wishes of his master, Mumba Zola. http://www.theizzystory.com/characters/the-bad/

The Earthlings: Thorf Serendopolis, Aristotle Maritimis, Carys Wynter, Illiachus Wynter, Thera, 1 Condor, Dee, Lisbet and Professor Devans.http://www.theizzystory.com/characters/the-earthlings/

The Good: The following characters in Iz~ The Izzy Story: Dorf Tzeus, Ponce Heidon, Chico Quwattle, Izzy Tzeus, Cimi Nuja, Kurl Tszargon, Robar Gimmel, and Phed: his legal name is *Skdjlsjflsjf Ilkjkld*. http://www.theizzystory.com/characters/the-good/

Thor: God of thunder and lightning in Norse mythology. Thor is said to be synonymous with the Celtic god Taranis.

Thor Heyerdahl: A Norwegian explorer and ethnographer who proved ancient peoples of South America were capable of sailing across the Pacific to Polynesia. He was Thorf Serendopolis' hero. See Ch. 4.

Time on Planet Authair: Planet Authair revolves around the center of gravity between two suns, Olym and Valym. One revolution of Authair is complete when it has reached its closest approach to a distant and third sun, Proxi. This is one Proxi cycle. One Proxi cycle is the equivalent of twelve Earth years.

Planet Authair rotates on an axis that is parallel to its axis of rotation around the center of gravity between Olym and Valym. This "daily" rotation creates another period of time that is measured in Olyms. Each "daily" rotation encompasses twenty Olyms. One Olym is equivalent to 100 minutes Earth time. Thus, each Authairian day is 33.3 hours long compared to 24 hours in an Earth day.

TLD—Procedure: Thermoluminescence dating is a technique used for determining the age of solids. It measures the accumulated radiation exposure of the object from the time it was formed to the present. See Ch. 3.

TLD—Spaceship: TLD stands for Thorium Lensing Device. Dr. D. D. Whatsus accidentally discovered the Lensing Energizing Mechanism while at graduate school working on his PhD. His discovery was immediately classified as top secret by the Authairian government. The Authairian Air Force developed the TLD as a means of traveling through space at previously impossible speeds.

Tookay: A puree of any fruit topped with a froth of gnarlythorn nectar. Jeeves must prepare a tookay of Dyzzleberry for Mumba Zola while on their trip following Graviton 1 to MBG21.

Tuna Broccoli Wafer: Izzy Tzeus's favorite food. See Ch. 1.

Vaccine Bubble Rolls: The storage containers for individual dosages of the ABMR-Virus medicine. Read about these in a future edition of IZ~.

Valympyon: A citizen of the hemisphere of Planet Authair that faces the sun, Valym.

Varrumph: Onomatopoeia for the sound that Graviton 1 makes when it enters and exits the dark energy field.

Villinois: A city in the Valympyon hemisphere famous throughout Planet Authair for its university. Chico Quwattle won a scholarship to the University of Villinois and earned a degree in biology.

Voice Stamp: A verbal pronouncement delivered by an authorized Authairian who seals a contract or commissions an action. You will read about this in a future edition of IZ~.

Wilco: The word used by flight controllers when they want to stress a point of compliance to the request of a pilot. It means, "will comply." You will read about this in a future edition of IZ~.

Selected Bibliography

These works represent the range of topics from which we have gleaned ideas to create our story, and they in no way make up our complete list of research materials. We have selected books, magazines and journal articles, DVD courses, and websites that we've found useful in developing the story over time. New sources of reliable and not-so-reliable information become available every day on websites around the world. We have recommended only those websites we feel represent well-established institutions and organizations.

Books

Asimov, Isaac and Robert Silverberg. *Nightfall.* New York, NY: Doubleday Publishing Company,1990.

Asimov, Isaac, *The Genetic Code.* New York, NY: The New American Library, Inc., 1962.

Barrett, John and David Iredale. *Discovering Old Handwriting.* Buckinghamshire, UK: Shire Publications Ltd., 1995.

Blascovich, Jim and Jeremy Bailenson. *Infinite Reality: Avatars, Eternal Life, New Worlds, and the Dawn of the Virtual Revolution.* New York, NY: Harper Collins Publishers, 2011.

Burrow, Steve, *Shadowland: Wales 3000 to 1500 BC.* Oxford, UK: Oxbow Books and Amgueddfa Cymru—National Museum Wales, 2011.

Cipriani, Curzio and Alessandro Borelli. *Simon and Schuster's Guide to Gems and Precious Stones.* New York, NY: Simon and Schuster Inc., 1986.

Coe, Michael D., Richard A. Diehl, David A. Freidel, Peter T. Furst, F. Kent Reilly III, Linda Schele, Carolyn E. Tate, and Karl A. Taube. *The Olmec World: Ritual and Rulership.* Princeton, New Jersey: The Art Museum Princeton University, 1995.

Cotterell, Arthur and Rachel Storm. *The Illustrated Encyclopedia of World Mythology: A comprehensive A-Z of the myths and legends of Greece, Rome, Egypt, Persia, India, China, and the Norse and Celtic lands.* New York, NY: Metro Books, 2010.

Darvill, Timothy. *Stonehenge: The Biography of a Landscape.* Stroud: Tempus, 2007.

Davaras, Costis. *Guide to Cretan Antiquities.* Ridge Park, NJ: Noyes Press, 1976.

Davaras, Costis. *Phaistos: Hagia Triada-Gortyn: Brief Illustrated Archaeological Guide.* Athens, Greece: Hannibal Publishing House, 1987.

Diehl, Richard A. *The Olmecs: America's First Civilization.* London: Thames & Hudson Ltd., 2004.

Donovan, Hedley. *The Celts: The Emergence of Man.* New York: Time-Life Books, 1974.

Ellis, Richard. *Imagining Atlantis.* New York: Alfred A. Knopf, Inc., 1998.

Flem-Ath, Rand and Rose. *In Search of Atlantis: When the Sky Fell,* New York, NY: St. Martin's Press, 1997.

Gott, J. Richard and Robert J. Vanderbei. *Sizing up the Universe.* Washington, D.C.: National Geographic Society, 2011.

Gott, J. Richard. *Time Travel In Einstein's Universe: The Physical Possibilities of Travel Through Time.* New York, NY: Houghton Mifflin Company, 2001.

Hamilton, Edith and Huntington Cairns. *Plato: The Collected Dialogues.* Princeton, NJ: Princeton University Press, 1961.

Hawking, Stephen W. *A Brief History of Time: From the Big Bang to Black Holes.* New York: Bantam Books, 1988.

Hodges, Henry. *Technology in the Ancient World.* New York: Barnes & Nobel Books, 1992.

Hughes, Arwel. *St. Fagans National History Museum Visitor Guide.* Cardiff: National Museum Wales, 2005.

Isham, Steven B. *Anoles: Those Florida Yard Lizards.* Orlando, FL: Commahawk Publishing, LLC, 2006.

Levine, Arnold J. *Viruses.* New York, NY: Scientific American Library A Division of HPHLP, 1992.

Marinatos, Nanno. *Art and Religion in Thera: Reconstructing a Bronze Age Society.* Athens, Greece: Mathioulakis & Co., 1984.

McNeill, John. *Old Sarum: English Heritage.* London: English Heritage Guidebooks, 2006.

Parker, Barry. *Cosmic Time Travel: A Scientific Odyssey.* Cambridge, MA: Perseus Publishing, 1991.

Pellegrino, Charles. *Unearthing Atlantis: An Archaeological Odyssey To The Fabled Lost Civilization.* New York, NY: Harper Collins, 1991.

Reader's Digest Writers. *The World's Last Mysteries.* Pleasantville, NY: The Reader's Digest Association, Inc., 1978.

Redknap, Mark. *Discovered in Time: Treasures From Early Wales.* Cardiff, Wales: National Museum Wales Books, 2011.

Renfrew, Colin. *Archaeology: Theories, Methods, and Practice.* New York, NY: Thames and Hudson Inc., 1996.

Richards, Julian. *Stonehenge: English Heritage.* London: English Heritage Guidebooks, 2011.

Robinson, Andrew. *The Man Who Deciphered Linear B: The Story of Michael Ventris.* New York, NY: Thames & Hudson Inc., 2002.

Robinson, Tara Rodden. *Genetics for Dummies 2nd edition.* Hoboken, NJ: Wiley Publishing, Inc., 2010.

Sakellarakis, J.A. *Herakleion Museum: Illustrated Guide.* Athens Greece: Ekdotike Athenon S.A., 2006.

Siegfried, Tom. *Strange Matters: Undiscovered Ideas at the Frontiers of Space and Time.* New York, NY: The Berkley Publishing Group, 2002.

Souden, David. *Stonehenge Revealed.* New York, NY: Collins and Brown Ltd., 1997.

Starr, Chester G. *A History of the Ancient World.* New York, NY: Oxford University Press, 1991.

Tzorakis, George. *Knossos: A New Guide to the Palace of Knossos.* Athens, Greece: Hesperos, 2008.

Vasilakis, Andoni. *Phaistos: Agia Triada Kommos-Matala.* Athens, Greece: Mystis, 2009.

Wilson, Colin and Rand Flem-Ath. *The Atlantis Blueprint: Unlocking the Ancient Mysteries of a Long-lost Civilization.* New York, NY: Delacorte Press, 2001.

Multimedia-DVD

Carroll, Sean Carroll, Professor. *Dark Matter, Dark Energy: The Dark Side of the Universe*, Course No. 1272: California Institute of Technology. Chantilly VA: The Teaching Company, 2007. DVD.

Filippenko, Alex. *Understanding The Universe: What's New in Astronomy: 2003.* Course No. 190: University of California at Berkeley. Chantilly, VA: The Teaching Company, 2003. DVD.

Garland, Robert, Professor. *The Other Side of History: Daily Life in the Ancient World,* Course No. 3810: Colgate University. Chantilly Virginia: The Teaching Company, 2012. DVD.

Harl, Kenneth W., Professor. *Origins of Great Ancient Civilizations,* Course No. 3174: Tulane University. Chantilly VA: Teaching Company, 2005. DVD.

Harvey, Hannah B., Professor. *The Art of Story Telling from Parents to Professionals.* Course No. 9313: University of North Carolina at Chapel Hill. Chantilly VA: Teaching Company, 2013. DVD.

Kelley, David E. *Picket Fences: Away in The Manger Season 3 Episode 10.* DVD. Studio City, CA: CBS, December 16, 1994. DVD.

McWhorter, John, Professor. *The Story of Human Language,* Course #1600: Manhattan Institute. Chantilly VA: The Teaching Company, 2004. DVD.

Zender, Mark, Professor. *Writing and Civilization: From Ancient Worlds to Modernity*, Course No. 2214: Tulane University. Chantilly VA: Teaching Company, 2013. DVD.

Magazines and Journals

Aron, Jacob. (2013, February 2-8). First Time-Travel Movies are Loopers. *New Scientist*, 8. Print.

Basri, Gibor. (2000, April). Discovery of Brown Dwarfs. *Scientific American*, 77. Print.

Cadigan, Pat. (2011). Cody. *trsf: The Best New Science fiction inspired by today's emerging technologies*, 27-38. Print.

Carroll, Sean. (2010, March). How to Travel Through Time. *Discover*, 40. Print.

Chown, Marcus. (2008, August 23-29). Land of the Rising Suns. *New Scientist*, 40. Print. Geddes, Linda. (2010, June). Me and my Avatar. *New Scientist*, 29-31. Print.

Gefter, Amanda. (2000, August 6-12). Beyond Space-Time. *New Scientist*, 34. Print.

Hambling, David. (2010, December). Wireless at the Speed of Plasma. *New Scientist*, 22-23. Print.

Heselton, Jill. (2011, January 21-27). TB We Can't Treat is Spreading in India. *New Scientist*, 8. Print.

Heselton, Jill. (2012, January 14-20). Milky Way Brims With Planets. *New Scientist*, 15. Print.

MacKenzie, Debora and Michael Le Page. (2010, December). Dawn of the Plantimals. *New Scientist*, 33-35. Print.

McKenna, Maryn. (2011, April). The Enemy Within. *Scientific American*, 46. Print.

Nicholls, Henry. (2011, September 10-16). Swarm Troopers. *New Scientist*, 34-37. Print.

O'Donoghue, James. (2010, December). Flight of the Living Dead. *New Scientist*, 36-40. Print.

Regis, Ed. (2010, March). The Picasso of DNA. *Discover*, 32. Print.

Seringhaus, Michael and Mark Gerstein. (2008, November/ December). Genomics Confounds Gene Classification. *American Scientist*, 466. Print.

Shiga, David. (2010, December). The Poison Eaters. *New Scientist*, 8-9. Print.

Sinha, Chris. (2011, October 8-14). Time. *New Scientist*, 37. Print.

Sivertsen, Sara and Henrik Elling. (2013, January/February). Top Ten: The Worst Epidemics and Diseases in History. *Science Illustrated*, 54. Print.

Tarlach, Gemma. (2014, January/February). Hunting a Killer Virus. *Discover*, 57. Print.

Vanderbei, Robert. (2014, January/February). Physicists Discover a Whooping 13 New Solutions to Three-body Problem. *Discover Magazine*, 46. Print.

Zorich, Zach. (2012, March/April). New Discoveries at Stonehenge. *Archaeology*, 14. Print.

Websites

Cartwright, Jon. Physicists Discover A Whopping Thirteen New Solutions to Three-Body Problem. *Science*. http://news.sciencemag.org/physics/2013/03/physicists-discover-whopping-13-new-solutions-three-body-problem. 8 March, 2013. Web. 26 Dec. 2013.

Cartwright, Mark. "Lyre." *Ancient History Encyclopedia.* THOHOST, 16 December, 2012. Web. 13, January, 2013.

Chenciner, Alain. "Three-body Problem." *Scholarpedia*, 3 October, 2007. Web. 13 January, 2014.

Hitt, David. "Exploration Beyond Earth: NASA Space Launch System Could Make 'Outside the Box' Science Missions Possible." *NASA.gov.* 14, January, 2014. Web 17, January 2014.

Suvakov, Milovan and V. Dmitrasinovic. "Synopsis: New Orbits for Three Bodies," *Physics.aps.org*, 8 March, 2013. Web. 19 January, 2014.

Wikipedia contributors, "Linear B," *Wikipedia, The Free Encyclopedia*, http://en.wikipedia.org/w/index.php?title=Linear_B&oldid=598676477 (Last modified on March 8, 2014).

Wikipedia contributors. "Accelerator Mass Spectrometry," *Wikipedia, The Free Encyclopedia*, http://en.wikipedia.org/w/index.php?title=Accelerator mass spectrometry&oldid=588011422 (Last modified on December 28, 2013).

Wikipedia contributors. "Allele," *Wikipedia, The Free Encyclopedia*, http://en.wikipedia.org/w/index.php?title=Allele&oldid=599037912 (Last modified on March 10, 2014).

Wikipedia contributors. "Stonehenge," *Wikipedia, The Free Encyclopedia*, http://en.wikipedia.org/w/index.php?title=Stonehenge&oldid=596053690 (Last modified on February 18, 2014).

Wikipedia contributors. "Thermoluminescence Dating," *Wikipedia, The Free Encyclopedia*, http://en.wikipedia.org/w/index.php?title=Thermoluminescence dating&oldid=596113915 (Last modified on February 19, 2014).

Wikipedia contributors. "Antikythera Mechanism," http://www.antikythera-mechanism.gr/ (Accessed on May 6, 2013).

Wikipedia contributors. "Brown Dwarf," *Wikipedia, The Free Encyclopedia*, http://en.wikipedia.org/w/index.php?title=Brown_dwarf&oldid=598822092 (Last modified on March 9, 2014).

Wikipedia contributors. "Cosmic String," *Wikipedia, The Free Encyclopedia*, http://en.wikipedia.org/w/index.php?title=Cosmic_string&oldid=593016133 (Last modified on January 29, 2014).

Wikipedia contributors. "Linear A," *Wikipedia, The Free Encyclopedia*, http://en.wikipedia.org/w/index.php?title=Linear_A&oldid=598680018 (Last modified on March 8, 2014).

Wikipedia contributors. "Polymerase Chain Reaction," http://en.wikipedia.org/w/index.php?title=Polymerase_chain_reaction&oldid=598987876 (Last modified on March 10, 2014).

Wikipedia contributors. "Prehistoric Wales," *Wikipedia, The Free Encyclopedia*, http://en.wikipedia.org/w/index.php?title=Prehistoric_Wales&oldid=572265312 (Last modified on September 9, 2013).

Wikipedia Contributors. "Neuroglia," *Wikipedia, The Free Enclyclopedia,* http://en.wikipedia.org/wiki/Neuroglia, (last modified on 8 September 2014 at 16:29).

About the Authors

Iz~ The Izzy Story is a joint creation between husband and wife. Ddwlem is the pen name chosen by D. Duayne Whitehurst and Lucille E. (Sandy) Mayton.

Duayne has a PhD in organic chemistry from The University of Iowa. He conducted research in petroleum chemistry and catalysis at the Central Research Division of Mobil Oil Corporation for 30 years. In 1979 he received the Henry H. Storch Award in Fuel Science for his contribution to the chemistry and utilization of coal. After retirement, he consulted for Mobil, Exxon, Chevron, and Merck corporations and was an adjunct professor at the University of Kyushu, Japan. Aside from his continued development of Iz~, Duayne maintains a long-enjoyed consultancy in catalysis and petroleum research with Haldor Topsøe A/S near Copenhagen.

Sandy holds a Master's Degree in Developmental Reading and has Reading Specialist and Supervisory Certifications from The College of New Jersey. Her professional career spanned thirty-one years in New Jersey as a teacher, a reading specialist, and an assistant supervisor of education. She enjoys bringing life to Iz~ in the various places the two of them call home. It may be in the southern United States, the northeastern United States, or Denmark where she and Duayne can be found, between family events, deep in the development and research of the next book.

Please visit them at http://www.theizzystory.com
If you enjoy the story please like them on Facebook at:
https://www.facebook.com/IZTheIzzyStory/

CPSIA information can be obtained at www.ICGtesting.com
Printed in the USA
BVOW10s1211021215

429135BV00008B/11/P

9 781941 536421